A French Finish

A French Finish

by
Robert Ross

G. P. Putnam's Sons, New York

SBN: 399-11884-5

Library of Congress Cataloging in Publication Data

Ross, Robert.
  A French finish.

  I. Title.
PZ4.R8252Fr   [PS3568.08443]   813'.5'4   76-48309

To PHM

A French Finish

Prologue

Graduation day.
Harvard.
Memorial Hall. June 13. Thursday.
Nicholas Otter.

Sitting with his "O" classmates, capped and gowned: O'Brian, O'Connell, Odell, Offenhaus, Olson, Orkin, Osborne, Ostreicher, Otter. Nicholas Otter, square-shouldered, still as a post, attentive.

Honorary degrees. Shrewdly chosen, as always.

Speeches.

"In your lifetime man split the atom, explored the surface of the moon, perfected the computer, network television, instant world communication. All in the past twenty-five years. You will live to see the year 2000. What will you be doing?"

I ought to decide what I want to do, thought Nicholas.

"Despite what you have been taught here, your brain does not search first for truth. It searches first for personal gain. Your brain, therefore, is the fang and claw of modern man. If you cannot deal with this reality first, your life will be very hard. Today this university has seen fit to bestow an honorary degree upon me. It did so, I suggest, because I am the chairman of the board of a company that manufactures and sells automobiles. Our corporate budget includes a very large endowment and annual contribution to this great school. We think it helps us to attract Harvard's best young people. Harvard needs our money. Both of us search first for our personal gain. Fang and claw, you see, even in the Ivy League. Very well. I accept the degree with thanks. Nevertheless, I understand the realities. Therefore, I know who I am. Do you know who you are?"

Yes, thought Nicholas, *I ought to decide who I am, too.*

"At Harvard you have prepared your mind. Have you also prepared your will, your spirit, your determination to achieve? Will you exercise your vital capacities? Will you pursue excellence? Will you move on to a field that gives you ample scope, so that you may apply your hard-won knowledge? Some will tell you that jobs are scarce and hard to find. Some will tell you that budgets are tight, and fat salaries are a thing of the past. You will be compelled to sit through difficult interviews and answer impertinent questions. Will your spirit bend? Will it break? Your degree from Harvard is a useful thing. But will you use it? Or will you turn to a rich father or to an influential uncle and choose the easy way?"

God helps orphans who help themselves, thought Nicholas.

"I have questions, but not answers. These you will have to discover for yourself and in yourself. I see only the shadow of the coming age. I will not live to see it. You will. For me the shadow moves slowly. For you it moves at a thousand miles an hour. I wish you well in your journey."

Applause; prompt, generous, rounded. Very Harvard.

The stately exit, two by two. Gowned penguins.

Parents.

Clusters of classmates.

Handshakes.

Who are you, Nicholas Otter?

I am an unemployed orphan with a Ph.D. in art history.

And what do you want, Nicholas Otter?

A job.

Ah. Bad luck.

One

She watched his tall, spare figure edge tactfully past a happy family that blocked the front doors like a maze. He's not really good-looking, Wren thought. But what the hell. He's tall and thin and grave and funny and gentle. Damn strong, too.

He saw her and lifted his diploma like a sword. She shook hers in reply and rose from the stone bench. She had been waiting for nearly two hours.

"Congratulations, Wren Wooding," he said, "Master of Fine Arts, *cum laude.*"

Congratulations, Nicholas Otter," she echoed, "Doctor of Art History, *magna cum laude.*"

"How does it feel to be a Master?" said Nicholas. He kissed her solemnly on each cheek.

"As a matter of fact, I'm a mistress," said Wren. "You made me what I am today. I hope you're satisfied."

"I'm satisfied," said Nicholas. "I happen to have a soft spot in my heart for tough little redheads named after birds."

"Damn few Harvard men have a Master for a mistress," said Wren.

"Damn few."

"Damn few graduates here today without fathers and mothers in tow, either."

"And brothers and sisters."

"And uncles and aunts and cousins."

"And grandmothers and grandfathers."

Wren laughed. "My mother isn't here because she thought my father would come. My father isn't here because he thought my mother would come. They don't talk anymore. It's the basic benefit of divorce, actually. What about you?"

"You mean from the County Home?"

"Sure," said Wren. "They raised you, didn't they? Fed you until you were as tall as De Gaulle. Told you to apply for your Harvard scholarship. Right? You've got to be their star orphan. Who was here?"

"Well," said Nicholas judiciously, "I did get a nice letter from Mr. Ragel. He explained that money was tight, as usual, and how the fare from Cincinnati was too much to spend. He was pretty blunt about the whole thing. It's the basic benefit of an orphanage, bluntness is."

"*Cincinnati?* This is the first time I knew that your Home was in Cincinnati. You never told me that before. Is that where they found you on the doorstep, wrapped in the Cincinnati *Enquirer?*"

"No, it wasn't like that."

They walked slowly through the little park, hand in hand. She came to his shoulder, barely. They strolled. From time to time Wren brushed her copper-red hair aside;

it hung, long and fine, to her shoulders. A short, slim figure, her head tilted. Wren listened.

He was seven. Mother and father dead in a sudden screech of brakes, crunch of metal. Memories blurred. Tears. Two plain caskets. Other fragments.
Small red bicycle.
Black dog with white paws.
Cloth bag of marbles that clicked when you moved.
Olive Street.
Middletown, Ohio.
The open grave.
The uncle. The uncle full of alcohol, full of himself, full of bachelor opinions, took him off to Cincinnati. His only relative. Uncle Walter the Salesman.
Two years later Uncle Walter died on a cold January morning. Massive stroke. Nicholas was alone.
Nearly ten.
The county did its duty. The Rhineland Home for Boys. Gray stone, black iron fence with spear-tip points, small lawn, beds of flowers in front, playground in back. Seventy-seven boys. The home fed them, clothed them, housed them, kept them busy at their tasks, punished them shrewdly, and saw to it that they went to school.
Brooms, brushes, mops, and rags. Sweep, scrub, wipe, and wax.
Wash, hang, iron, fold.
Dining tables covered with white oilcloth. Set and clear.
Pots, pans, plates, bowls, cups, glasses, knives, forks, spoons. Wash, rinse, dry, put away.
Broken furniture to be mended.
Faulty sockets to be repaired.
Lawns to be cut.
Flowerbeds to be weeded.

Gray paint for the front door. Clean the brushes.

Lights out at nine if you are under twelve.

Lights out at ten if you are over twelve.

If you spit, how to you expeck-ta-rate?

NO SECONDS.

Seventy-seven boys. Seventy-six who built their days around a ball. A baseball. A basketball. A football.

One boy, Nicholas Otter, cleaned the attic when he was ten and discovered a wooden box, nailed shut. A set of the *Encyclopaedia Britannica*. Edition of 1929.

That was the way it started.

"Jezuzz," said Wren, "what a fantastic husband you're going to make. Do you realize the range of your talents? You really mean you can do *shirts*?"

"I worked it out once. I could be a janitor, waiter, electrician, house painter, gardener, plumber, dishwasher, and laundromat king."

"Goddamn few Harvard men can make that statement," said Wren.

"Goddamn few."

"And I've known you for two whole years, and you never once hinted at this fantastic background," said Wren. "You've been holding out on me."

"Not really. I wanted to wait until we'd been graduated. Besides, we've gotten to know each other pretty well."

"I know," she said complacently. "We made love. Counting last night, we made love three hundred and twenty-eight times in the past two years."

Nicholas stopped and peered down at her. "You've been *counting*?"

"Bet your ass I've been counting. I've been looking for trend lines."

"Trend lines?"

"Certainly. For instance." Wren frowned and collected

16

her thoughts. "For instance. You're better in the winter than in the spring. You tail off—and I *mean* tail off—in the summer, and begin to pick up around September. You're better on weekends than on weekdays. You're more imaginative on weekends, too."

Nicholas shook his head. "I don't believe this. You make it sound like an IBM marketing report. I never knew you were keeping track."

"So I never knew about Cincinnati. You tell me your secrets, I'll tell you mine. The way I see it, we're a perfect fit. You can do all those neat things around the house, and I can keep track of how we make love. It's a hell of a base to build a marriage on, if you ask me."

"I don't need a wife. What I need is a job."

"That."

"That." Nicholas thrust both hands deep into his pockets and kicked moodily at a small stone. "I've got my degree in art history, sure. Now, how do I use it? Teaching? Not a chance. Schools aren't hiring; they're cutting back. Ditto museums, ditto galleries, ditto the big private collectors. Ditto, ditto, ditto. So what would you like to marry? An orphan who can't find a job as a teacher, or an orphan who can't find a job as a museum assistant? You want to know the state of the world? Up to its ass in unemployed art historians. *That's* the state of the world."

"I think you have to have a job before you can lose it, so you can go on welfare," said Wren.

Nicholas shook his head. "You have to try to understand the orphan mentality," he said. "Welfare is worse than stealing. It's like legalized self-pity, and orphans use up their supply of self-pity at a very early age. I didn't sweat my way through Harvard so I could get married and apply for food stamps to feed my wife. No way. What I need is to use my head in a job that's got some juice in it. And juicy jobs are goddamn hard to find."

"I know. I've been to the placement office maybe sixteen times. The way it stands right now, I can be a stenographer for a plastics-extrusion company in Long Island City for forty-five hundred dollars a year. That's if I can type eighty words a minute and take dictation."

"Nobody dictates to Wren Wooding," said Nicholas calmly.

"Bet your ass."

"So I've got my degree. Unemployed art historian. Wren, *what the hell am I going to do?* What are *you* going to do?"

She nudged her shoulder against his arm. "You're a big thing, and you have nice pale agate eyes, and from September to June you are a fabulous lover. But there are moments when you forget the fundamentals. You follow me. I'm going to give you your graduation present, and you are going to give me mine."

He studied her face for a moment, then smiled. "Three hundred and twenty-nine?"

"Maybe three hundred and thirty, too, if we put our minds to it. After all, it's still June."

"Right," said Nicholas. "I'm coming."

"Not yet," she said, "but soon."

Two

Wren stretched and yawned prodigiously, flexing her toes, then wriggling them. "You think too much," she said.

"I think all the time," said Nicholas. "Except when we make love."

"That's what I like about you. You treat me like a sex object. Delicious." She kissed his shoulder. "Get me the cigarettes, will you please? I can't move."

He rolled out of the valley in the center of her bed and padded across the room to the chest of drawers. The mirror on the wall caught his eye.

"I look eminently employable," he murmured. He bent closer, studying his reflection intently. "Consider the nose. Thin, yes. But inquisitive. Large, but not unreasonably large. Just the kind of nose a museum should be looking

19

for. Good jaw, too. Firm, but not stubborn. Goddamn jaw is better than the nose, if you ask me."

"What I asked you for were the *cigarettes.*"

"The face is a shade on the thin side. The hair is sort of dirty straw. I concede that. On the other hand, who wants to hire a fat face with hair like *clean* straw?"

"The matches are stuck in that little clock."

He scaled them across the room and followed after, carrying the cigarettes and a small ashtray. "Never mind my face and my jaw and my hair. I have to decide who I am and what I want to do, and I have to decide *soon*. The year 2000 is coming at a thousand miles an hour."

"What the hell are you talking about?"

"That's what this car salesman said at graduation. Who are you? What do you want to do? That's the thing." Nicholas stared into space. "They gave him an honorary degree. Damn good man."

"Harvard gave an honorary degree to a *car* salesman?"

"Sure. He said my brain is fang and claw."

"Jezuzz. What a speech."

"That's what he said. My brain is my weapon. We can't use clubs and rocks anymore, see?"

"If I'm following this, your brain is your fang and claw. Right?"

"Right. It hit me like a brick on the back of my head, honest to god. I've been using my brain like a goddamn filing cabinet. Damnit, Wren, it's a *weapon!*"

Wren laughed softly. "You knock me out. Twenty-four years old, and you announce the discovery of your imagination!"

"Laugh," he said sourly. "What I've got is a sort of stainless-steel scholarship brain. I read things. Then I remember them. Then I write a paper or take a test, and it all comes oozing out. Facts."

"What kind of facts?"

"The stylops, for instance. Goddamn little twisted-wing parasitic fly. The male stylops mates with the female sty-lops, who lives in the abdomen of the honeybee. So here's the damn bee, digging its nose into some flower, and mean-while, at the bee's backside here's this goddamn stylops banging away at the lady fly *inside* the bee."

"Wow."

"My head is full of stuff like that. Useless. Who the hell *cares* how Trebizond got its name, or what the barber to King Midas whispered into this hole in the ground? I mean, who *cares?*"

"A fly that bangs a bee in the ass. Fantastic."

"I listened to this car salesman, and I tell you, Wren, my brain went sort of all white and glowing, like in *Fantasia.*"

"Really? Then what happened?"

"This little Turkish pasha came tiptoeing out of my mind."

"A little Turkish *what?*"

"Pasha, pasha. A fat, greedy, sybaritic little son of a bitch, full of demands. He wants a pink pearl and a golden goblet and champagne. The pearl is for the wine. For the bouquet. That's what he says."

"Got it. Inside, you have this pasha."

"Right. He wants a black Rolls-Royce with a little luggage rack up on the roof, and those big round headlights with the metal louvers. He wants a motor yacht. Crew of four-teen with a freezer for grouse and venison and lobster. He wants a plane. An Apache or a Comanche. And a private pilot."

"The pasha in his Apache. I like that." Wren hitched her-self to the edge of the bed and stretched out her hand. "Where's the ashtray?"

"He wants a cottage in the Cotswolds with a thatched roof, and a flat in London in Belgravia. He wants an apart-ment in New York at 80 United Nations Plaza. He wants a villa in Positano. All these places have to have servants who live there, waiting for us to appear."

"Us?"

"Me and the pasha."

"Ahh-*ha*. And what about Ankara?"

Nicholas looked at her blankly. "What about Ankara?"

"Well, it's in Turkey, Pasha Nicholas."

Nicholas shook his head. "No, he didn't say anything about Ankara."

"I'm going to get dressed," said Wren. "The sun is going down, and I want some food. Shall I help you, or do pashas dress themselves?"

"What it boils down to," said Nicholas softly, "is that I need to make an enormous amount of money."

In the soft dusk of twilight they walked slowly along Massachusetts Avenue and into Harvard Square.

"This Turkish pasha," said Wren. "Did he talk to you while we were making love?"

"I think so," he said. "It was sort of subliminal. When we hit our orgasms, I did blank out, I know that."

"Like trying to keep your eyes open when you sneeze," said Wren. "Reflexive. You can't think when you're having one. Not even a Harvard man."

"It was only for a few seconds. Then the pasha came back with more demands."

"A dozen shirts, each with eight diamond buttons?"

"That sort of thing."

"A solid-gold filing cabinet."

"No. But I'd like my own personal chef. Or . . . or my pasha would."

Wren smiled for the first time. "You were beginning to worry me. I'll tell you my hunch. If Princeton offered you a job as an assistant instructor in art history for nine thousand dollars a year, I think you would drown your pasha in a barrel of honey and grab it."

"You just don't understand orphans," said Nicholas. "I've got to make it big. *Big* big." He shook his head moodily. "Let's get some dinner. I'm hungrier than I've been in years."

Wren tore a corner from the paper packet of sugar and tilted some into her coffee. "I'd like a cigarette now, please," she said.

"The point is that I've been using my brain all wrong. My head is packed with facts, and my bank account is just about empty. It has to be the other way around." He tapped the table emphatically. "What I need is a base. A bankroll. Seed money. Cripes. I wish I had a rich father."

"For a loan?"

"No, *hell*. If I had a rich father, and if he died tonight, and if he left me fifty thousand dollars in his will, I'd be set. It happens."

"You're an *orphan*, doctor."

"So I'm an orphan. We leave the restaurant and I meet this crusty old Boston tycoon outside. I help him across the street. Touched by my innocent courtesy, he asks my name. Bang. He rewrites his will, and I get a green tin box full of shares in U.S. Steel."

"I think it happened to James Stewart. I saw it on the late show, once."

"Or maybe I win one of those contests. Twenty-five thousand dollars a year for life and all the peanut butter I can eat. Something like that."

"Listen," said Wren, "they offer enormous rewards for the capture of these international criminals, don't they? Go catch one of those and turn him in."

"There's money in oil," said Nicholas reflectively, "but

you have to own one of those nutty Arabian countries first."

"I bet the Louvre would pay a fortune if you came in with the missing arms of the Venus de Milo. Why not dig them up?"

"Dive. You'd have to dive for them. They're sunk in the Aegean Sea somewhere. I'd do it, but I loaned my submarine to a casual friend. He never brought it back."

"Anyway," murmured Wren softly, "I don't worry about you. You may have a head full of facts, as you say. But pretty soon you'll hit your foot on one you can use. You'll be fine."

"You're smoother than baby powder," said Nicholas, "and very good for my morale. But the reality is this. I have eight hundred and seventy dollars in the Shawmut Bank. It nails me to square one, and square one is where you sink." He shook his head. "Sink, sank, *sunk.*"

"I have forty thousand dollars I can put my hands on," said Wren. "Maybe more."

Nicholas placed his coffee cup back onto the saucer. "Say that again."

"Give me a match," said Wren, "and I'll talk."

They sat on the steps leading to the entrance of the Fogg Museum. Moonlight dusted the building.

"Clocks and coins?" Nicholas said again. "You have forty thousand dollars' worth of *clocks and coins?*"

"Not just clocks and coins, Nicholas," she said patiently. "Very rare old clocks and very rare old coins. My grandfather had this famous collection. The James Jefferson Wooding Collection. It was in *Time* magazine once. Anyway. He left me part of it—a very small part of it—in his will. It was valued by the appraiser at forty thousand dollars, and that was ten years ago. It has to be worth more now."

"And you're willing to sell it so I can have a bankroll?"

"Well. I'm willing to sell it . . . so that we can go into partnership."

"Partnership?" Nicholas blinked and shook his head. "Doing what?"

"You need seed money to make a great big killing so you can make your pasha happy. Have I got it straight?"

He nodded.

"I agree," said Wren.

"You want to make an enormous amount of money, too?"

"Well, that. But I want to shut that goddamn pasha up," said Wren. "He gets in my way."

Nicholas stared out over the dark campus. "Where do you keep this collection of clocks and coins?" he said at last. "In some safe-deposit box?"

"Hell, no. In my room."

"You keep a forty-thousand-dollar collection in a dormitory room?"

"It's only two clocks and three coins, Nicholas."

"That funny little old-fashioned brass clock on your bureau—the one with matchbooks sticking out all over it?"

"That's not brass, doctor. Solid gold." She thought a moment. "At least, the case is. It's a Pinchbeck."

"A *what*?"

"Christian Pinchbeck. You can see his name engraved on the base plate. And the date. Seventeen twenty-eight. It was appraised at ten thousand dollars, I think."

"Clocks and coins. One thing they didn't teach me at Harvard was clocks and coins. Can I take a look at them?"

"Certainly. We'll look at the clocks and coins, and then we'll go to bed again."

"I don't know," said Nicholas. "Do you think partners ought to go to bed together?"

"It's clause one," she said.

* * *

The two small clocks and the three coins, lined up neatly on the desk, gleamed golden under the lamplight.

"They're impressive," Nicholas murmured, "once you know they're gold. But they sure as hell don't look like forty thousand dollars' worth."

"That's because you don't understand collectors," said Wren. "If it's rare, they want it. If it's in good condition, they yearn for it. But if it's expensive, they'll move heaven and earth to *own* it. Then they sit and look at it and *gloat*."

"Gloating is the big thing, eh?"

"Really."

"This one. It's only a three-dollar gold piece." Nicholas squinted at the tiny coin. "Eighteen seventy-five."

"They minted twenty that year. Six are lost. In the whole world there are just fourteen of these. This is one of them."

"Why only twenty?"

"Well, it wasn't a very popular denomination, and they had hundreds of thousands of three-dollar coins in stock from previous years, all unused."

"So because it's an 1875 it's valuable?"

"I think the appraiser said about five thousand dollars' worth."

Nicholas returned the tiny coin to the desk and picked up the large golden coin next to it. "Looks like the face of some Caesar. From ancient Rome, right? Must be two thousand years old and worth a *fortune*."

"More like two hundred years old, partner. It's what the appraiser called a Becker."

"What's a Becker? Or . . . who?"

"Carl Becker. He forged some marvelous copies of old Roman and Grecian coins. From gold and silver. They're very well made. Fooled the experts for years and years."

"Fake?"

Wren nodded cheerfully. "If it was genuine and in that

kind of condition, it might bring a hundred thousand dollars—or more. As it is, a Becker is an expensive little collector's curiosity."

"How expensive?"

"Haven't the faintest idea."

Nicholas reached for the third and final coin. It alone
was displayed inside a trim little plastic box resting in a
fitted velvet nest. "I wouldn't open it if I were you," said
Wren. He studied the coin more closely.

"A fifty-dollar gold piece. Eighteen fifty-four. *Why*
shouldn't I open it?"

"Because as long as it's in mint-perfect condition, it's
worth maybe twenty thousand dollars. If you drop it or
dent it or scratch it—boom. There goes five or ten thousand dollars. They minted only two of these, partner. It's
very, *very* rare."

"You *are* crazy," said Nicholas heavily. "Suppose you
were robbed? What if you misplaced this stuff?"

"Oh, they're safe. I've had them here at school for five
years, right? I keep them wrapped up in an old bathing suit,
and who the hell steals old bathing suits? Nobody."

"Anyway, tomorrow we can talk about turning these
things into cash. You know how to do that?"

"Easy. We take them down to New York and give them
to the biggest and best auction gallery in the city."

"Gilliat's?"

"Gilliat's. I have my grandfather's letter proving they're
mine to sell. I have the appraiser's documents made out to
me. I bring it all to Gilliat's, and they put the clocks and
coins into one of their catalogs for a scheduled sale. They
send out the catalogs, and all the dealers and collectors
come in and bid. We'll sell it all."

"Even the Becker?"

"Oh, sure. Someone always wants one, even as a
curiosity."

Nicholas picked up the big golden coin and rubbed the ball of his thumb softly over the surface. "Fang and claw," he mumbled.

"What?"

"You got a Kleenex?" said Nicholas.

"Certainly I've got a Kleenex. What the hell for?"

"My Turkish pasha thinks we ought to hold on to the Becker for a while. I want to wrap it up in a Kleenex."

Wren shook her head. "Here's two. What the hell. Be a plunger. Does your Turkish pasha say *why* we should hold on to the Becker?"

"Not really."

Wren stretched. "I'm tired." She yawned. "I've had a tough day at the office, actually. Undress me, will you please?"

"I get the soft pillow for a change," said Nicholas.

"You pashas are all alike," said Wren.

Three

The gracious old landmarks of New York town are dissolving, like a doomed sand castle. The waves of boom and build, decade by decade, have cut away most of the lovely churches of honest red brick, washed away all the great old inns, the stately homes, the sprawling, brawling markets. A few of the neighborhood squares are left— sternly fenced and locked. There remain a bare handful of cobbled mews—closed to traffic. And of the old, old trees, with trunks so thick you could not put your arms around them, none stands.

Well, yes, Lüchow's restaurant hangs on, full of dark woods, oom-pah music, and stag heads, stuffed and glassy-eyed. Bits of Coney Island still survive, they say. And Gilliat's. The auctioneers.

Gilliat's stands stubbornly in its rightful place, down at the lower end of Fifth Avenue. It is surrounded now by button wholesalers, artificial-flower distributors, and narrow little stores filled with novelty goods from Taiwan.

It was there one hundred years ago, in the same four-story building of impossibly ugly mustard brick, and there wasn't a single one of New York's best families who couldn't find the way to Gilliat's blindfolded.

Harlan Gilliat started it all in 1870. Down from Boston he came, with seven wagons piled high with Sheraton furniture, fine bone china, old silver, bronzes, Chinese porcelains, rugs, tapestries, three suits of Italian dress armor, and eighteen "French paintings"—each one framed in intricately carved woods, gilded and shining.

He hired the grand ballroom in the best hotel in town and announced, with seductive modesty:

A PRIVATE SALE

By Invitation Only

FINE ANTIQUES
Each one imported from the collections
of CERTAIN DUKES AND DUCHESSES of Central
Europe and now offered to the
LADIES AND GENTLEMEN of New York by
Harlan Gilliat of Boston Town, Mass.

Harlan Gilliat aimed to sell to the best people. "The best people have the most money," he would say in his dry Vermont voice. And he was full of ideas.

Right from the first, the Gilliat's auctions were conducted on a far higher plane than the common shoutings of the time. For one thing, each of Gilliat's customers sat on an armchair of red velvet, padded and comfortable. And Gilliat's guaranteed everything, including complete satisfaction, for a full year. So that if customers tired of a January purchase in February, they knew they had until December to make their returns and get a full refund, no questions asked. Very few did, true enough. But the subtle reassurance lubricated many a wavering bidder, just as the comfortable chairs kept them there, ready to bid again. As Harlan had intended.

Even at that historic first sale, Harlan's auctioneers, like the items they sold, were imported. British to a man, perfectly groomed, utterly calm, they never raised their mannered voices, never pleaded for just one more bid. They made Gilliat's famous overnight. Bids, even those most frantically signaled, were always acknowledged with the merest nod, the tiniest dip of the chin. Within weeks New York's most powerful nabobs were to be observed making their iron wills known in the same fascinating fashion. That minute nod of approval, Gilliat's personal invention, caught on and spread like a brushfire.

In every way, Gilliat's first sale broke new ground. It sent Harlan hurrying back to Boston with his seven wagons, his mind churning with plans to fill them up again. He traveled to England and to France, to Italy and to the Low Countries, his pockets full of hard cash, always skimming the cream, skimming the cream.

In time, the mustard-brick building rose, floor by floor. At the street level were displayed the items to go on sale in the following weeks. Here too came the first trickle of treasured collections to be sold; it was soon to grow to a flood of books and prints, paintings and sculptures, furniture and bibelots; a never-ending river of offerings. For a percentage, Gilliat's sold the best of it.

The second floor, where the sales were held, had a low stage at the back of a long, narrow hall seating just four hundred. Offices were housed on the third floor, and storage rooms filled the top floor. All in all, a way-station sort of building, designed to take in old antiques at one end and change them into dollars as they moved out at the other. A simple building, it made Harlan Gilliat rich.

It was on the second floor where a single Rembrandt drawing sold for the then record price of sixteen thousand dollars. The year was 1889. From the same podium on the same stage came the world's first two-hundred-thousand-dollar bid. It was made, and accepted by that tiny nod, for "The Contents of a Gentleman's Library"—the gentleman in this case a very bankrupt railroad magnate with a superb collection of first editions. That was in 1901.

Harlan Gilliat watched it all with beady-eyed concentration and taught his growing staff of buyers to make friends of the impoverished nobility of Europe and skim the cream. "When they need money, pay them a good price and skim the cream," Harlan would tell them. "Let our competitors buy the leavings."

He lived long enough to see many of these best things return, at the owner's death, as part of the Gilliat Estate Sales; and he died in 1904, wise and wealthy and full of years. He left four sons, who produced, in their turn, six more. At Gilliat's, you dealt with Gilliats. But sons or no, it was Harlan's spirit that watched over the enterprise and guarded the flame.

His visage, clean-shaven, remarkably contemporary, looks at you, open-eyed and bland, as you enter the front door. It is a Mathew Brady photograph, sturdily framed in plain oak, and it carries a small bronze plate along the bottom:

HARLAN GILLIAT

1830–1904

OUR FOUNDER

So Gilliat's stands.

The building is unchanged. Not even an elevator found its way into that stubborn structure until 1940. The atmosphere remains—a comfortable blend of one hundred years of dust, wax, and old money. And the center of it all, the hub, the heart, the essence of Gilliat's, is the Sale Room.

"Can you smoke in here?" asked Wren. They stood in the doorway at the rear of the empty room, staring at a sea of chairs.

"My God, look at this place," said Nicholas. "Those hanging lightshades are Tiffany glass, I think. I mean, real Tiffany glass. They sell *copies* for two hundred dollars. And look at that table. It's as heavy as a truck. It must be a thousand years old, and they keep sale catalogs stacked on it."

"I don't see any no-smoking signs," said Wren. "I think you can smoke, but I don't see anybody smoking. In fact, I don't see anybody at *all*."

"Too early," said Nicholas. "The morning sale at Gilliat's starts at ten-thirty. We've got forty-five minutes." He surveyed the room. "Let's sit in the back."

"Why the back? We'll be able to see more and hear better up front."

"Back here we can see who the bidders are. If we sit up front we'll have to twist around all the time, and you'll miss the auctioneer. Maybe at the side along that wall is better, about three-quarters of the way back."

"They have ashtrays attached to the seats," said Wren. "I think I'll have a cigarette. It's the last one in the pack, but I'm nervous."

By ten-twenty-five the room was about one-quarter filled. Nicholas came back up the stairs and through the door, sidling down the length of the aisle to his seat. "Dealers, mostly. Antique dealers." He lowered his voice. "The regulars."

"How do you know that?" asked Wren.

"Pinkerton guard downstairs; I asked him. Day in, day out, eighty percent of Gilliat's crowd are the regular dealers. Plus a few sellers who show up, like us. A few tourists sometimes, he says. Mostly in July and August. Sometimes a secret agent."

"*Here?*"

"Somebody nobody knows, who represents a big museum or maybe a big private collector. Rich buyers want to keep well out of sight, because the prices get pushed up if the dealers recognize them. So they send a buying agent."

"I thought you went down to the men's room."

"I did. But I got to talking with this Pinkerton guard."

There was a small stir at the front of the room as a heavy green curtain was drawn back to reveal the rear wall, its shelves arrayed with the items to be sold. Two elderly men in gray coats came through the door at the side of the stage and moved idly to the shelves, consulting a typed list from time to time and whispering. Then two young men walked slowly across the stage to seat themselves at the low table to the left of the podium.

"One of them records every bid," whispered Nicholas. "The other one takes in the money."

"Pinkerton research?"

Nicholas nodded.

"Who's *he?*" asked Wren.

From the door, the tall figure of a man emerged, his Anthony Eden face lordly in its composure. He walked with a bishop's dignity to the podium that stood like an altar, front and center stage.

"Piers Shaw-Alcott," said Nicholas softly. "The senior auctioneer."

"He looks English."

"He is English," said Nicholas, "because all of Gilliat's

auctioneers are one hundred percent English. Shaw-Alcott is probably a hundred and thirty-two percent English."

At the podium the auctioneer slid an elegant wrist a discreet inch out of his perfect sleeve to consult his watch, then extracted an ivory cube from a small box and held it three or four inches above a larger block of polished ebony. From somewhere offstage a low chime sounded, and with it, the ivory cube clicked once against the wooden block.

"Good morning, ladies and gentlemen. We present an assortment of odd lots today in July Sale Number Sixteen. Standard conditions of sale shall apply, and may we have Lot One, please."

He paused as one of the gray-coated aides stepped forward, carrying a small ornamental inkwell. He held it high above his head, turning first to the left, then to the center and the right, to give all present a fair view.

"Lot One, a gilt-metal and porcelain inkwell," Shaw-Alcott intoned, "the blue celeste holder with floral panels, a gilt-metal lid on a wavy base. Late nineteenth century, five inches wide, five inches high, four inches deep; we will start at fifty dollars. May I hear your bids?"

There followed an almost invisible exchange of tiny nods, slow blinks, and finger lifts, all of which Shaw-Alcott monitored imperturbably.

"I have seventy. Thank you."

"I have eighty."

"I have one hundred."

"In the back of the room I have one-twenty."

"I have one-fifty."

"And one-sixty."

"I have two hundred."

"I have two-ten."

A pause broke into the flow of bidding, and the senior auctioneer lifted his ivory cube, repeating, "I have two-ten.

Done?" The brief nod. The ivory cube clicked. "Two hundred and ten dollars to Mr. George Weisbrod of Bounty Antiques." His golden pencil made a brief notation. The whole business had taken less than a minute.

"May we have Lot Two, please?"

Wren shook her head. "Unbelievable. Two hundred and ten dollars for that thing."

"You have to understand collectors," said Nicholas. "Weisbrod knows a collector who needs that inkwell, probably to complete a set. He'll sell it for four hundred and fifty dollars or something, and the collector will take it home and set it on the table and look at it and *gloat*."

"So I've heard," said Wren dryly. "What lot number are we, again?"

"One hundred and twenty-one. We're third from the end."

"I'm going across the street to buy a pack of cigarettes. Mind the store till I get back."

"Je-*zuzz*," said Wren. "*Seventy thousand dollars!*"

"Seventy-one thousand, two hundred and thirty dollars," said Nicholas serenely. I missed it by . . . um . . . five thousand."

"You thought we'd get five thousand less?"

"No, no; five thousand more. I thought your fifty-dollar gold piece would go for at least five thousand dollars more. But I hit your Pinchbeck clock right on the nose."

"Thirty-two thousand."

"Right. That's what I had down here."

"You've been studying clocks and coins, haven't you?" said Wren. "You're trying to protect my money, Nicholas Otter. That's very nice."

He leaned over and kissed her on the ear. "I am beginning to sniff my way along a trail that will make you a very rich woman, Wren Wooding. And as you prosper, so shall I."

"Anyway, that's the bankroll. What now?"

"We wait. Gilliat's will take off their ten percent and send you a check in a few weeks."

"Well," said Wren slowly, "I'll try to think of some ways to make the time pass."

Four

"Do you know how many times we've made love in the last three weeks?" said Wren bleakly. "Three times."

"I've been very busy," said Nicholas.

"Saturday night. You show up on Saturday night, like for some goddamn bowling-league date." Wren punched the pillow, then punched it twice more. "Three times in three weeks; no good. I am a very strongly sexed woman, Nicholas. We've *got* to do better than three times in three weeks."

"The check from Gilliat's came yesterday."

"Right. I endorsed it. You deposited it."

"Then, I've been talking to people and thinking and visiting some museums."

"You've been visiting some museums, Nicholas, but museums close at five-thirty. They're not open all night—and I *am*."

"At night? I've been reading some books and making some notes and going to some meetings."

"What kind of books and notes?"

Nicholas let his eyes wander. "Oh . . . different kinds of books and notes."

"What *kind* of meetings? And with *whom?* Look, Nicholas, I *know* you. You're brewing up some plot to make a million dollars, and it's turning me into a goddamn sex-starved shrew. I'm all tensed up, Nicholas." She threw a quick glance at him. "Queer thing happened to me yesterday. Your Turkish pasha began to talk to *me.*"

"You're kidding."

"I'm serious. He thinks we ought to have a bedroom in all our houses with a ceiling that's one big mirror."

"What the hell *for?*"

"So I can look up and see more than your nose hairs."

"That doesn't sound like the pasha," said Nicholas.

"He also thinks I should have a dimmer switch on the side of the bed, right where I can reach it."

"To turn the light off?"

"To turn the light on, Nicholas. Otherwise, how can I see the mirror?"

"I thought you wanted to shut the pasha the hell up," said Nicholas.

"Not in my goddamn condition."

"Well. Pack a bag. We're going back to New York for a few days. You are about to turn from a sex-starved shrew into a very active partner." He paused, his eyes glinting. "I think I've got an idea," he said softly.

Wren gave a short yelp of happy surprise and hit him softly on the chest. "Damnit," she said, "you've been toying with me, haven't you? Lie down. It's only Thursday, but what the hell."

Five

"Why are we going to New York by *bus*, for god-sake," said Wren, "when we've got seventy-one thousand dollars in the bank?"

The Greyhound moved smoothly along the broad highway. Next to the window, Nicholas watched the tailored fields and neat frame farmhouses slide by, his lips moving in some silent calculation.

"We could have rented a car," said Wren. "Je-*zuzz*, we could have *bought* a car. And it takes one hour by plane. Less."

"Sixty-four thousand, one hundred and six dollars," said Nicholas.

"What?"

"That's what we had in the bank. Sixty-four thousand, in round figures."

"Ahh-ha. Gilliat's took their ten percent."

"Correct."

"And what do you mean, that's what we *had* in the bank? Don't we have it anymore?"

"Not exactly. Not for thirty days, anyway. I rented it out."

"What's that supposed to mean?"

"Commercial paper. I put the money into commercial paper. The bank does it. We get ten percent. We make a profit of about five hundred dollars in thirty days."

"Where did you learn that stuff?"

"My roommate last year. His father sent him *The Wall Street Journal* so he'd give up medieval manuscripts and go into banking or something."

"Jiggs Cronin."

"Yep."

"So you read *The Wall Street Journal* and learned about commercial paper, and Jiggs read his medieval manuscripts, and we're going to New York by bus. Got it. Where did you get the money for the bus tickets?"

"I still have eight hundred and seventy-four dollars in the Shawmut Bank. I used some of that."

Wren leaned toward him and combed his hair with her fingers. "You're working hard to protect my money, Nicholas. I like that."

"That's clause two. Besides, it takes longer by bus, and I've got a lot to tell you."

"At last it comes out. What the hell *have* you been doing these past three weeks?"

"Recruiting."

"Recruiting whom? For what?"

"And research."

"All right. Researching what? For whom?"

"It all goes back to that Becker of yours. Now, let me talk, and you sit there and listen." He closed his eyes for a moment. "I'd better start with the research."

* * *

The Gilliat windfall had stunned Nicholas, literally. That otherwise ordinary human beings would bid aggressively to pay more than seventy thousand dollars for two small clocks and two golden coins struck him with the force of something akin to a mystic revelation.

One hundred and twenty-four items had been sold that morning, for just under five hundred thousand dollars. Ivory fans and astrolabes, enameled snuffboxes and painted inkwells, bun-shaped paperweights and Delft pottery, their own clocks and coins, and one improbable rattail spoon that was bid up and up again and again until it was knocked down for nearly four thousand dollars. Four thousand dollars for a spoon! Nicholas marveled. But the Pinkerton guard had called it a fairly dull day. Come back for one of our Evening Sales, he had said indulgently, when one item will go for half a million dollars and more.

Like Harlan Gilliat, Nicholas returned to Boston Town, his mind churning. Clearly, there were enormous sums of money floating around in this heady new world. How to tap into it, how to tap into it? Questions seethed in him.

He made his first probe into the prosaic shelves of a little branch library in Cambridge, and like Schliemann's inspired discovery of the treasures of Troy, struck pure gold almost at once. No matter what you wanted to collect, there was a book to tell you how. Not one book, indeed, but many.

What did people collect? Only everything.

How long had it all been going on? Only forever.

Two thousand years ago, wealthy Roman senators collected rare old Grecian coins.

Three thousand years ago, proud citizens of Athens collected Egyptian antiquities.

Six thousand years ago, pharaohs made certain that their

treasures from Nineveh and Tyre were buried with them.

There was a lust to collect, with roots deep in the human spirit; a hunger to own, to find, to possess. The appetite extended even to buttons and badges, dolls and matchbook covers, meerschaums and toby mugs, mechanical banks, toy trains, lead soldiers, coins, books, bottles, serpent jewelry, campaign posters, arrowheads, armor, decanters, snuffers, medallions, keys, clocks.

Nicholas pored over *Mighell's Guide to 800 Toothpick Holders,* full of wonder.

And, oh, the struggles of the Vanderbilts and the Morgans, the Astors and the Depews! How they collected, and how they bought! And what of old imperial Hearst, bidding for whole Spanish castles and buying them, down to the smallest dish in the last cupboard. Tycoon pitted against tycoon, iron will against iron will, to own the one delicious Goya, the one Gutenberg Bible, the one Alba Madonna. Five hundred thousand dollars would be bid, then six. Seven. Eight. Nine. The crowded auction room would go still as dawn's hush, while eyes gleamed and glared and the silken voice of the auctioneer went from one stubborn leviathan to the other, until the million-dollar bid sounded in the room like an oratorio.

"Westchester," said Wren. "I think I'll have a cigarette."

"As it turns out, every collector has one problem," said Nicholas.

"*That's* encouraging."

"Most of the time, demand is bigger than supply."

"So it pushes the price up. Right?"

"Hmm? Yes. It does that. But that's not the problem. The problem is, Wren, that there's always a Mr. Becker hiding in the bushes."

"Becker? *My* Mr. Becker?"

"Your Mr. Becker. I thought a lot about him. Back around 1820 there were lots of rich collectors who wanted rare old Roman coins—but with damn few on the market. So Mr. Becker made a mint."

"Clever. He made a mint, so he could make a mint. A counterfeiter."

"They've been around for as long as collectors. And that's the real problem. The fear of buying a fake. It tortures every collector, every museum, every gallery."

"Fake coins I can see," said Wren, "but fake *toby mugs?* Fake *dolls? C'mon."

"Believe it. *Whatever gets collected gets faked."*

"You're getting ready to tell me something," said Wren. "Why don't you just say it?"

"We're going to make a perfect copy of a very rare antique and sell it as the real thing," said Nicholas gently.

"That's a crime, isn't it?"

He nodded, his face empty of expression.

Wren stubbed her cigarette into the ashtray, doing it slowly, crushing each fragment of the burning tip. "Well," she said, "it isn't exactly what I had expected, but every partnership needs a policy. We're for crime. Is that it?"

He nodded again.

She tilted her head and closed one eye. "I guess you had better tell me why," she said.

"I'm going into business for myself. You're a partner. It's that simple. I didn't work my way through Harvard so I could be poor."

"But criminals *cheat* people, Nicholas. I don't think Harvard had that in mind, actually."

"Not a problem. The way I'm planning, it's going to be a victimless crime. Do what I did, Wren. You think back to Carl Becker. Whom did he cheat? Think about it. I mean, *really* think about it."

A French Finish

* * *

Carl Wilhelm Becker. Born 1772, died 1830. His golden counterfeit fascinated Nicholas. True gold, gleaming and heavy. He would turn it over, rubbing his thumb softly over each surface. True gold. Counterfeit. True gold. Counterfeit. But it was nearly a century after his death that the Keeper of the Coins and Medals of the lofty British Museum finally published the exposure of the Becker counterfeits—a hundred years too late, thought Nicholas.

Somehow, the fakers flourished. One of them sold a wax bust "by Leonardo da Vinci" to the Kaiser Friedrich Museum in Berlin. Another sold "genuine" letters from Mary Magdalen to Lazarus. Alceno Dossena sold "ancient" Greek sculptures to the best museums of the world, and Hans van Meegeren sold magnificent Vermeers that passed every scholarly test. When passion seized the collector and his heart raced, he was deaf to reason, and blind. He wanted to believe. He believed.

He bought the first eight chapters of the book of Genesis, suitably aged in tobacco juice, of course.

He bought medieval footstools, bright with shining nail-heads where wooden pegs should be.

He bought antiquities of dynastic Egypt, still damp from Nile clay.

There was nothing the collector would not buy.

There was nothing the faker would not copy.

Well, well, Nicholas concluded solemnly. We must ponder deeply of Carl Becker and his work. Yes, indeed.

True gold.

Counterfeit.

"In other words, quality crookery is our policy," said Wren. "You do understand that you might go to jail?"

"Not if it's worked right," said Nicholas.

"Come to think of it, I might go to jail, too."

"Only if we get careless or greedy, or if we talk too much."

"I've never been in the slammer," said Wren, "but as I listen to you, I get the uneasy feeling that the boys in the cellblock talk a lot like you."

"No problem. If you want out, you are out."

"And you?"

Nicholas narrowed his eyes and stared calmly out of the window. "I told you. I'm going to make a copy of a very rare antique and sell it for a great deal of money. Then I'm going to do it again. I've thought it all out; the main lines of it, anyway. It's my new career." He turned and brought his face close to hers. "Listen to me. I'm an art historian, and a goddamn *good* art historian. Out there in the world are lots of unemployed teachers and damn few jobs. If I can't work as a teacher, if museums have no openings, if collectors won't hire me, if galleries have no jobs, then what should I do? Take a job selling men's underwear at some big department store and wait for something to happen? No way, Wren. No way. Becker made fakes out of solid gold. Beautiful fakes. That's what I'm going to do. Harvard got me ready. That's *it*."

"No jail?"

"No jail."

"I can have my money back?"

"Every dime. In thirty days, that is. With a five-hundred-dollar profit. I'm willing to start with what I've got, if I have to."

Wren pulled a hand across her face. "The George Washington Bridge. This goddamn bus is moving too fast. Do I have to give you an answer right now?"

Nicholas grinned and kissed her lightly on the eyebrow. "Certainly not. I'm taking you to Gilliat's to show you the first project. After you see it, we can talk some more. Then you can decide."

"We're going to Gilliat's now? They close at five, don't they?"

"As a rule, yes. Not tonight. Tonight is the Evening Sale," said Nicholas.

Six

It has been a significant social event for at least a century, the lineal descendant of those famous sales first organized by Harlan Gilliat himself. No more than two are held each year, and every ticket is ardently pursued.

There are several aspects of the Evening Sale that set it apart. For one thing, the press is invited; they sit in their own reserved section, hung with cameras and portable tape recorders, confirming the atmosphere of significance. The famous interior decorators also appear—narrow-faced men who talk like women, or heavy-thighed women who look like men—their dazzled clients in tow. The Old Money never misses these proceedings—men of affairs who come with toothy, opinionated wives, and their checkbooks, prepared to buy. But the smaller dealer, source of Gilliat's daily bread and butter, is nowhere to be seen in this caviar-and-champagne setting. In his place stroll the stately princes of the dealer world, older men, most of them, with smoother, pouchier faces and colder eyes. Tonight they will match bids with anyone in the room.

The Evening Sale also brings a useful scattering of delegates from Zurich, Rome, Paris, London, and elsewhere; they make their bids in charming accents and, invariably, spur certain Americans on.

It is Gilliat's design to make each item in the Evening Sale one of major importance; to this end, months are spent culling and gathering the rarest, the most delectable of the treasured antiques of the world. Which brings, as might be expected, the museum trustees and their acquisitions directors, the scholars, the pundits, the savants, and the critics.

The comfortable armchairs are removed, to be replaced by narrower folding chairs. This adds one hundred more places, but seating is always desperately inadequate. Therefore, at the Evening Sale Gilliat's will abandon one of their traditions and allow the overflow crowd to stand along the walls, or at the back, or even at times, on the platform itself.

Nicholas held two tickets, and it had taken a deal of doing. The Pinkerton guard, enlisted as an ally, had taken the application in hand and—indulgently—steered it through Gilliat's processing labyrinth, monitored by an iron-faced secretary named Mrs. Gosset. Thus, in due course, two tickets went into the mail. "The sale starts precisely at eight on Tuesday evening," Mrs. Gosset had written, "and we suggest that you plan your trip from Boston so as to be here at least one-half hour in advance."

Nicholas and Wren sat now, as before, in the same location—by the far wall, about three-quarters of the way back—and watched as the room slowly filled. At the table flanking the podium, four young men were on duty tonight to record bids and arrange the completion of each sale. Behind them, six gray-coated porters moved in and around a great muddle of furniture: chairs, tables, desks, cabinets, sideboards, footstools, all compacted and internested like some enormous jigsaw puzzle.

A low hum filled the room, a sound akin to the stirring of the hive as the bees inside make ready to sally forth. Mr. Shaw-Alcott, the master beekeeper, already at his post, watched and waited. From time to time, he knew, one of his bees might sting. But he would harvest honey this night.

A chime sounded, calling the murmurous room to instant silence. Mr. Shaw-Alcott clicked his ivory cube.

It was time.

"Good evening, ladies and gentlemen. The Evening Sale will offer sixty-six lots of furniture from England and the Continent. You will find them listed in this sale catalog, number twenty-two." The senior auctioneer held it up for all to see—a thin booklet with Gilliat's dark brown baroque border. "I am told that it helps a bit to have one of these at hand. Do let us know if you care to have one."

Soft laughter rolled over the room. Follow Gilliat's Evening Sale without a catalog? Unthinkable! How amusing of old Shaw-Alcott. How droll.

"On the platform tonight we have managed to find room for twenty-seven lots. As they are sold, they shall be removed, and the rest of the lots will be brought in. You see," said the auctioneer, leaning forward on the podium as though to impart a confidence, "if we have to bring all sixty-six lots into this room . . . well, we'd be hard put to find a place for *you* to sit, wouldn't we? And that wouldn't do at all." More soft laughter; the auctioneer studied its sound with an ear trained by a thousand jousts, and liked what he heard.

"May we have Lot One," he said, turning to the porters.

"What the hell was that all about?" said Wren.

"Stroking," said Nicholas, without turning his head.

"Warming up the rubes?" said Wren. "Unbelievable."

"Shut up," said Nicholas, "and listen to the bidding."

"Screw the bidding. What number are we waiting for?"

But Nicholas only shook his head. The buyers were aggressive tonight; bidding had leaped swiftly from the auctioneer's call for a starting bid of one thousand dollars for "a pair of ebony-wood chairs, inlaid with equatorial woods in a sun-ray motif on the back and with finely turned saber-legs." The chairs stood alone under the spotlight, two English horrors from the late eighteenth century, already bid to eleven thousand dollars. Moments later they fell to one of the tweedier interior decorators, bidding for her tense client and winning—at twelve thousand, two hundred. The race was on.

Two porters at once moved forward to remove the chairs, while two more replaced them with a small mahogany table. "A Sutherland table, Lot Two," said Shaw-Alcott, "with D-shaped flaps, raised on heavy, spiraled twist-turn legs." While the opening bids were called, one of the dealer-princes strolled nonchalantly to the platform and lifted one of the little side flaps, kneeling to study the construction. When he rose, dusting his knees, the bidding had already reached nine thousand dollars. He stared at Shaw-Alcott and nodded.

"And ten from Mr. Bookbinder."

". . . and eleven. Eleven I have."

"And twelve from Mr. Bookbinder."

"And thirteen."

"And *fifteen* from Mr. Bookbinder."

At this signal of determined intent, the opposition collapsed, and at fifteen thousand dollars the tea table was sold. The first stirring of real excitement came about twenty minutes later, when a small chest of drawers appeared. "A very fine Goddard-Townsend piece, the only American item in our sale tonight, it is dated 1776 and is an excellent example of shell-carved decoration. We will begin the bidding at seventy-five thousand dollars."

Nicholas," hissed Wren, "this is *killing* me! Is that the first project we came to see?"

Nicholas shook his head. First came four quick bids, from four parts of the room, each of ten thousand dollars. The rhythm slowed as the five-thousand-dollar bidders moved in, pushing the price to one hundred and sixty thousand. Now, cautiously, the one-thousand-dollar bidders surfaced.

"One-sixty-eight I have," said Shaw-Alcott placidly. He paused. "One-sixty-eight I have," he repeated. Silence filled the room.

". . . and *done.*" The ivory cube clicked down. "One hundred and sixty-eight thousand dollars to Mr. and Mrs. Roger Pelham. May we have Lot Twenty-five, please?"

"Two to go," said Nicholas. "This next one, and one more. Then . . ."

Wren's eyes raced down the page. "Twenty-four was just sold," she muttered. "Twenty-five next, then Twenty-six. Then Lot Twenty-seven. *Ahhh* . . ." Her finger traced the lines of the text, which read:

Lot Twenty-seven: *Bureau du Roi—Louis XVI.* Signed by Oeben/Riesener. Dated 1771. In characteristic marquetry. Very fine.

"That's *all?* A *bureau du roi?* What the hell *is* it?"

Nicholas rolled the catalog into a little tube and put it to his lips, touching Wren's ear with the other end. "A sort of writing table," he said softly.

"What's so special about it?"

"Look," said Nicholas.

It was, Wren saw at once, a superb expression of the furniture art. Standing alone, under the lights, it conveyed an elegant sense of balance, of wholeness, of perfect integrity of line. Perhaps five feet wide and three feet deep, it made everything that had preceded it seem suddenly quite ordinary.

"That's it?" said Wren. "That's the project?"

Nicholas nodded. "What do you think of it?"

"Wow."

". . . an exceptional piece," Shaw-Alcott was saying, "with marquetry in mother-of-pearl, tortoiseshell, ebony, and ivory. It bears the signatures of Jean-François Oeben and Jean-Henri Riesener and is dated 1771." He paused to survey the room with a benevolent eye. "We will open the bidding at four hundred thousand dollars," he said.

Wren's eyes went round as dimes. The auctioneer's voice tolled out the bidding for two minutes, perhaps three; the porters moved forward to lift the writing desk away, and it was done.

"Six hundred and eighty thousand, four hundred and fifteen dollars," said Wren. "Je-zuzz!" She bumped her shoulder against Nicholas and said intensely, "I'm in-in-*in.* If we're going to forge a copy of something, let's at least get six hundred and eighty thousand dollars out of it!"

"Lower your voice!" Nicholas hissed.

She winced and looked around her. No one had heard. "It's only *sensational,*" she whispered. "My god, I like the way your head works!"

"Right," he said softly. "Then you're in. You are now the third member of the Becker Gang. Welcome, Redbird."

"Redbird?"

"Your code name."

She grinned happily. "I've got a code name." She straightened up suddenly. "The *third* member of . . . of the Becker Gang? What gives?"

"I think it's time for you to meet the professor. Let's get the hell out of here. We're flying back to Boston tonight."

"The professor? *What* professor?" But Nicholas was already moving down the aisle toward the exit. "Redbird," muttered Wren. In her haste she stepped heavily on the foot of one of the attentive bidders.

"Excuse me," said Wren. "I've got to fly."

Seven

"This is where he lives," said Nicholas.

It was a narrow wood-frame house, very old, painted a dark gray, with white shutters and a white door. It sat modestly behind a small front yard, screened by three or four oak trees and a thick hedge of lilacs. On Faculty Row, a ten-minute walk from Harvard Yard. Number 30.

They mounted the steps. In the center of the door there was a small roundish brass affair with a well-worn turner at its center. Directly above it a white card displayed a name in curly Gothic script. Wren leaned forward and squinted.

"Lewis Poe Tewksbury," she murmured. She looked up at Nicholas, chewing on her lower lip. *"Professor* Tewksbury? *He's* in the gang?"

Nicholas twisted the little handle, and they listened to the sound of the bell. There was a brief moment of waiting. Then the door swung open.

"Good morning, Nicholas. And this must be Miss Wooding! Come in, my dear, come in! So nice to see you both. I've made a pot of tea."

He's *old,* Wren thought. Thin. Really thin. And nearly as tall as Nicholas. Silvery white hair, silvery white eyebrows, silvery spectacles. Lots of wrinkles. Nice handshake; firm and easy.

"I like your looks, too," said the old man.

"You're quite a surprise to me, Professor Tewksbury. Nicholas wouldn't tell me a thing. You're his secret, I guess."

"Very rightly," said Tewksbury. "Your young man has a nice sense of priorities. But we meet at last. Let's sit in the parlor and talk, shall we? No more secrecy, Miss Wooding." He moved down the long center hall that divided the house, then opened the last door on the left. "You would like some tea, wouldn't you?"

"And a cigarette," said Wren. "Is it all right if I smoke?"

There were, Wren saw, several impressive rubber plants, glistening with health. Broad green leaves grew to the ceiling from pale blue Chinese ceramic pots that were festooned with twisting dragons and gold ornament. A window box of ferns ran the length of the room; rattan furniture was neatly arranged around a large hempen rug. A silver teapot and some cups and saucers sat on a table. Through the window Wren could see a pleasant little garden, dominated by a red maple tree aglow in the corner. It made a pretty picture.

"I planted that tree myself, forty-six years ago," said the old man. "It was a sapling, and so—alas—was I. It was four years old, and I was . . . um . . . thirty-four."

"Almost fifty years ago," said Wren. "That's pretty old." She turned from the window and sat beside Nicholas on the small sofa. Tewksbury lowered himself into the rocking chair. It squealed as he leaned back, squealed again as he rocked forward, settling in.

"It is a long time," said Tewksbury, nodding. "That old tree and I grew up together at Harvard. But we survived. In all fairness, one does owe them that much." He pursed his lips together and made a sour mouth.

"Owe whom? What happened?" said Wren.

"Retirement, Miss Wooding. Retirement happened. Terrible, terrible thing, retirement. The Harvard people extended the mandatory limit by a year, I concede that. But they added a deadline with the extension. The Dead Line. An awful idea. I suppose I should have died to simplify things. I remember there was a farewell luncheon and a scroll and an invitation to use my old office for a year. But it was over." The old man rocked back and forth restlessly. "Well. I had no intention of dying, I can tell you that. Nor, I think, do you blame me, eh?"

Wren shook her head.

"Oh, no, no blame at all. If it's living or dying, living is definitely better. There's . . . there's more to *do*."

"Precisely my own reasoning. One would say instantly that there's more to do. But it isn't that way at all. The facts are that I had no classes to teach, no meetings to attend, no seminars, no papers—*nothing*. A very bad situation, I can tell you."

"You spoke at the Weber lectures last year. I was there."

The old man frowned. "The Weber lectures. Blether. Once a year I find a form invitation in my mailbox. It names the day, date, time, and place and gives me forty minutes. Forty minutes! My students used to say that I needed ten minutes just to clear my throat." He shrugged ruefully. "Quite true, you know. I *like* to ramble."

"Is there an ashtray here, please?" said Wren.

"Naturally, I did what was expected. People were always

most kind. They insisted on helping me up the stairs like some damn nonagenarian. But they meant well . . . and it did bring me back to the campus, if only for one day."

"I think I'm getting it," said Wren. "You didn't have enough to do . . . and Nicholas figured that out." She beamed at Nicholas. "That *was* smart."

"It wasn't quite that way," said the old man dryly. "We seemed to haunt the same sections of the same libraries. And one day we began to chat. Our Nicholas is an exceedingly cautious fellow, Miss Wooding."

"I know," said Wren. "But I'm having a hard time understanding something. You're a famous professor. I mean, really famous. I've seen your face on the cover of *Time* magazine at least twice. In other places, too. Famous people are always busy, aren't they? Being famous, I mean."

"My fame. Yes, I'd nearly forgotten about that. Someone discovered a painting in an attic in Rome, and a committee of brainless fools promptly certified it as a long-lost work by Michelangelo. They actually placed a value of fifteen million dollars on it. Imagine! An insurance syndicate at Lloyds asked me to look at it, and so I did. It was quite old, of course. But no Michelangelo, not at all. The magazine decided that it made for a good story. That was years ago. So much for fame. Blether!"

"There it is again," said Wren. "What's blether?"

"Bullshit," said the old man serenely. "Blether is simply plain old-fashioned bullshit."

"That's very cool, you know?" said Wren, turning to Nicholas. "Really." She thought a moment. "What about the Federal Arts Commission thing? Doesn't that keep you busy?"

"Ah yes," said Tewksbury, "the other *Time* cover story. Last year I wrote a letter to the editor, proposing a national arts commission—elevated to cabinet rank and status. The sort of thing Malraux did in France, you know. *Time* sent an intense young woman here to interview me, and a young man with three cameras and very bad skin. He took hundreds of pictures. One of them went on the cover, much to my surprise, I may say. But it left the main problem unsolved. A man cannot keep busy waiting for *Time* magazine to come calling, if you see what I mean."

"It's your face," said Wren suddenly.

"Yes," said Tewksbury at once, "I quite agree. The public seems to enjoy pictures of certain very old faces. George Bernard Shaw has been dead for years. Bernard Baruch, Cordell Hull, Grandma Moses, Robert Frost, Casey Stengel—all gone. But they still have me, you see. I'm told I bear some resemblance to a film actor. He's gone, too, poor man. William Huston, was it?"

"Walter," said Wren. "Walter Huston. John Huston's father. It's true, too. You do look a little like Walter Huston."

"I daresay. Of course, my hair is a good deal whiter, and I've more lines on my face. It makes me look like a sage, no doubt. But it's hardly enough to keep a man active." He leaned forward and poked Wren twice on the knee. "White hair or no, inside I'm not seventy-nine. I promise you that."

"Eighty," said Nicholas mildly. "I read in *Who's Who* that you were born in 1896. That makes you eighty."

"Not for five months," snapped the old man. "I'll be eighty on my next birthday, and not before."

"But not inside," said Wren.

Professor Tewksbury nodded vigorously. "Not inside." He tented his long fingers and spoke softly. "The body of my work was complete twenty years ago. Sixteen books, you know. A Pulitzer Prize for one of them. Not bad, not bad at all. But I've said everything I want to say. I think my work will stand with Vasari and Pater and that nice little man Berenson. And I did rescue two Vermeers and an Ucello. I'm quite proud of that."

"I've read your book about the fake Rembrandt drawings," said Wren.

"Have you?" The old man looked pleased. "I wrote that a
long time ago, Miss Wooding. In the early forties. Yes,
many of the major museums used to send me all sorts of
works when they were in doubt. That's how the so-called
Rembrandts came my way. It rarely happens anymore.
Once in a very great while an old friend of mine will ask me
to come down to New York to look at something at one of
the dealers . . . or to advise him on a bid for something at
Gilliat's." He smiled at Nicholas briefly.

"That's how Nicholas and I began to talk, in fact. We ran
into each other at the museum one afternoon."

The enormous painting, done in the grand French manner, showed Louis XVI, surrounded by an adoring court. It
hung from ceiling to floor, virtually covering the wall. Nicholas knelt to study an object shown in the lower corner.

Two black shoes appeared at his knee, and the now familiar gray flannel trousers. Nicholas sighed and craned his
head, peering up.

"Not again!"

"Coincidence number four, isn't it?" whispered Professor
Tewksbury. "Wonderful brushwork on the lace cuffs. Have
you noticed it? From ten feet away the lace effect seems
photographic. Yet, up close, see how cunningly his brush
deceives our eye. A few lines, crisscrossed; no more. Quite
marvelous."

"You followed me from the library this time. Right?"

"Guilty, Mr. Otter."

"You got my name from the librarian?"

"Guilty again."

"You waited for me in the section on period furniture last
week. Right? I guess it's time to find out why, professor.
Frankly, you're getting on my nerves."

They sat side by side on the low padded bench facing the great painting. At the end of the long, narrow gallery a uniformed guard glanced at them briefly and yawned.

"Out first meeting *was* a coincidence, Mr. Otter. It was, in fact, a small miracle. I remember I'd left my wallet at home. I had to go back for it, of course. It delayed me just enough to bring me to the library just as *you* went through the front door. You were carrying a copy of one of my own works; naturally, I was interested. Do you remember which one it was?"

Nicholas nodded.

The old man winked. "I thought you might. *Detection and Validation of Art Forgeries,* wasn't it? You caught my eye, young man."

"So you started to spy on me?"

"It wasn't only my book. You showed an unusual interest in antique fakes, copies, replicas, reproductions, I must say. It puzzled me. It intrigued me. After all, I *am* retired. Time hangs heavy, and so on. And then . . . my juices began to bubble!"

"Your . . . juices?"

"It began to grow on me that you were planning something illegal! What a thrill went through me! Here I was, withering up like an old prune . . . and along comes the smell of adventure! Adventure! By god, my juices began to bubble. Do you follow?"

"You think I'm planning something illegal . . . and you're attracted?"

"You've spent hours and days and weeks studying fake antiques. How to make them, detect them. Who collects them, exhibits them, trades in them. You've been to the law library, reading cases on antique fakers who've been taken to court. I've kept fairly close to your trail, Mr. Otter. *You're up to something . . . and I'm fascinated.*"

"You're . . . fascinated."

"That I am. I'm not *sure* what you're planning, mind you. But it strikes me that I might be of some help to you. Before you say anything, Mr. Otter, consider that I might blow the whistle if you turn me down."

Shock washed over Wren's face. "You mean you *blackmailed* your way into this gang?"

"That I did, Miss Wooding. That I did."

"But you'll be a *criminal*. What about that?"

A long, slow smile lit up the old man's face. "I hope so, Miss Wooding. I hope to be quite a *good* criminal, and it doesn't bother me one damn bit. Making a copy of that little writing table is a superb idea." He rubbed his hands together slowly. "Better, in fact, than you realize. As for me, I wish to atone for the sin of too much education. When I was thirty I knew that life ought to be an adventure. Then I spent forty-six years unlearning that priceless bit of wisdom. My dear young woman, dishonesty has a tradition quite as old as honesty's—and frequently more distinguished. As for collectors, they *love* to be deceived. It gives them something to talk about, you see."

"What about your . . . your reputation?"

Tewksbury shook his head. "I'm like the forty-year-old virgin. I'm tired of it."

"What about the risk? Policemen, jail, trials, convictions, all the sordid publicity? Doesn't that bother you?"

"Do you really believe that Lewis Poe Tewksbury will be suspected, my dear? With my sixteen books? My white hair? My patriarchal visage? Come, come. I'm perfect camouflage!"

"A Pulitzer Prize front man," said Wren.

"Would *you* arrest Walter Huston?" said Nick.

Wren sighed. "Inside, the professor here is a thirty-year-old adventurer. Inside, you've got this goddamn Turkish pasha. And I've got sixty-four thousand dollars in the bank. Is that it?"

"The Becker Gang," said Professor Tewksbury solemnly.

"And I'm Redbird. What's the professor?"

"I'm Yardbird, Miss Wooding. From Harvard Yard, you see? I chose it myself. Quite apt, don't you think?"

Wren grunted. "There are yardbirds and there are yardbirds," she said, "but never mind. And you, Nicholas. What kind of bird are *you*?"

Nicholas smiled slyly. "I'm the only leader we've got, so I took a title. I'm the Admiral Byrd."

They looked at her expectantly. After a moment she took a cigarette from the pack. "Redbird to Admiral," she intoned. "Need a match . . . repeat, need a match. Over and out."

"Right," said Nicholas. "We go to work."

"One thing you mentioned sticks in my mind," said Wren. "*Why* is this Louis XVI table a better idea than Nick realized?"

Tewksbury nodded approvingly. "Ah, yes. The heart of the matter, Miss Wooding. There are hundreds of kinds of art and antiques that Nicholas might have chosen—all of which would have been exposed as fraudulent in a matter of minutes by any one of a whole battery of modern testing methods." He ticked some of them off, one by one, on his fingers. "X rays, of course. Fluoroscopy. Spectography. Chemistry. Carbon-14 dating. Raked light. Many more. And you have no idea how accurate these devices are. They simply cannot be fooled. Well. Our little table will be delightfully immune to every test there is!" He smiled slowly. "Quite immune."

"But why?"

"Let's consider the wood, my dear. We need woods that

are two hundred or so years old. Difficult, yes, but not at all impossible. The materials for the decorations, the inlays, and the marquetry are readily available—the mother-of-pearl, the ebony, the tortoiseshell, and so on. As for the varnishes, the waxes, and the glues—why, the original craftsmen were kind enough to leave us carefully written recipes. Indeed, we'll be able to use their own drawings and notes. Both Oeben and Riesener were consummately precise workers."

"What were they, exactly? Partners?"

"Hardly. Oeben was a German cabinetmaker who became a Frenchman and went to work for the great Charles Boulle, who died in 1754. As did Louis XV. The new king, Louis XVI, made Oeben his *Ebeniste du Roi*—cabinetmaker to the king. Oeben promptly hired Jean-Henri Riesener—another transplanted German—as his assistant. They worked together for seven or eight years, when Oeben died. A few years later Riesener married Oeben's widow, inherited all his tools and drawings, and in due course was himself appointed *Ebeniste du Roi*. Now, pay attention! In those seven or eight years when the two men worked together, creating together, designing together, producing together, an odd custom arose. Oeben began to allow Riesener to sign many of their works!" The old man's eyes glinted. "I leave to your lively imaginations the difficulty this presents to modern scholars and experts who hover over the outpouring of magnificent furniture signed by Oeben or Riesener . . . or *both*! Who did this one? That one? Who designed this? Who made that? It makes for a lovely puzzle. But it gets even better. Much better." He sipped from his cup of tea, smiling. "After Riesener married Oeben's widow, he continued to sign his own works with Oeben's name, as well as his own! Did the widow insist on it? Was it sentiment? Or did Riesener hope to profit from the continued association with his old master? No one really knows. But it makes a marvelous muddle for the experts who try to date the work or identify the maker. Of course, we've learned to identify one characteristic that was specifically Riesener's—a sort of special refinement quite his own."

"What kind of refinement?"

"You must try to remember what the king's court was like in those days—spiderwebs of treachery and intrigue and secret cabals! Spies and counterspies were everywhere. Small wonder! It wasn't too many years later that they cut off the poor king's head . . . and Marie Antoinette's, too. So his majesty gave certain instructions to our friend Riesener. He wanted concealed drawers, hidden panels, hidden compartments that no one else would know about. There he could preserve his most private documents from prying eyes, you see. These cleverly concealed hiding places are not to be found on any of the original designs or drawings. But little by little, over the centuries, they *have* been found, of course. Sometimes a hundred years later! Our friend Riesener was a genius at these little refinements, no doubt about it. And for us, his genius is like manna from heaven."

"I'm missing something," said Wren.

"Of course," said Nicholas softly. "We'll need documents never before known, proving the authenticity of our desk. And where will they be found?"

"In one of those secret compartments," whispered Wren. "What a fantastic idea!"

"Quite," said Tewksbury. "My thought, precisely. What could be more natural than to find a sweet love note from Marie Antoinette to her royal spouse? A line or two of a naughty reminder of the pleasures of the regal bed, perhaps . . . and a casual line expressing the hope that her beloved sovereign will enjoy the little *bureau du roi* she has ordered Riesener to make for him. Especially the marvelous secret compartments!"

"I love it," breathed Wren.

"When I show you how artfully Riesener concealed his tiny drawers and compartments, you'll love it even more, my dear," said the old man. "Rococo and baroque are styles alive with swirls and curves and intricate marquetry. I will point out the precise location of a Riesener compartment, Miss Wooding, and challenge you to find it—or open it."

"The designs for our desk," said Nicholas. "Can we get them?"

"Indeed we can. We'll find designs very much like ours in several scholarly papers. They'll be most useful. But when you chose that *particular* table, Nicholas, it was a stroke of genius!"

"Why so?"

"For two reasons. First, that table happens to be one of at least four. All virtually identical. All authenticated. All discovered unexpectedly at various times over the past two hundred years. So that the appearance of our table—signed by Riesener and bearing Oeben's name—will not offend the experts. It's happened before, they will say. It has happened again!"

"And the other reason?"

"Ah, yes. Better still! In Paris, at 23 Rue de Sévigné, you will come upon the Musée Carnavalet. A fascinating little museum that holds the odds and ends of Parisian history. Hardly ever visited by tourists. A most charming and informal place. It was an elegant town house, actually, back in the 1500's, a gathering place for the fashionable nobility of Parisian society. There are twenty-seven rooms in the original building. In later years the adjoining houses were added, so that it must have sixty or seventy rooms now. Pictures, of course. Quite a lot of furniture. China, silver, glass, books, marvelous old wrought-iron tavern signs, street signs, old city maps, a good deal of material on the Bastille and the various French revolutions. And, as you would expect, quite a nice little . . . um . . . reference room. You'll find the complete set of drawings for our table there. It's quite private. And there's a copying machine in the corner. Convenient, wouldn't you say?"

"How do *you* know all this?" said Wren. There was awe in her voice.

"I've used the museum many times, my dear. All part of the job, you know."

"You Harvard professors are too much," said Wren. "We ought to recruit ten more and take over the Mafia and run it as it ought to be run. So all we do is go to this museum, make a copy of the drawings, and walk out. Is that it?"

"You'll need a letter from someone they know. A customary formality."

"Like you, say?"

"No," said Nicholas quickly. "We want to keep the professor behind the bushes, out of sight. It'll have to be someone else."

"Professor Broudage, then," said Tewksbury. "Miss Wooding should arrange to see him. He's at the Sorbonne, and he likes attractive young women. You need tell him only that you are interested in interior design and decoration, I should think."

"That's it, then," said Nicholas. "After that, we'll need your master cabinetmaker, professor. Greedy, crooked, and willing to keep his mouth shut, right? Professor, tell Redbird here about Caspar."

"We'll find him in Bruges, Miss Wooding. Caspar Van der Ek. Just our man. Quite greedy, I assure you."

"How greedy is *quite* greedy?" said Wren.

"He'll want at least twenty-five thousand dollars," said Tewksbury, "but he'll ask for much more at first."

"Twenty-five thousand. We can handle that," said Wren. "*How* crooked is your Mr. Caspar Van der Ek?"

"Like a corkscrew, my dear. I once came very near to

having him put away for ten or fifteen years. He tried to fox some museum friends of mine. It was quite a long time ago, but he'll remember me, I'm sure. Indeed he will. He was most grateful when I agreed not to press charges. We're old friends, he and I."

"And he'll keep his mouth shut, won't he?" asked Wren. "For twenty-five thousand dollars, I mean?"

"So we hope. But it's best to move very carefully with Caspar."

"We'll go to Paris," said Nicholas, "and get those designs first. Then, Bruges."

Eight

"Fantastic city," said Wren. "Why don't more people know about it? Practically no tourists."

"It's nearly November," said Nicholas. "Bruges is supposed to be a madhouse in the summer."

"And so it is," said the professor. "It's a wonderful city, you know. Canals like Venice, twisty streets like Florence, old stones like Rome, monasteries with paintings by da Vinci—and only six miles from the beaches and the casinos at Ostend and Zeebrugge. Tourism is the only real industry Bruges has now."

They sat in the lounge of the Hotel Portinari, huddled around a tiny table, their second cup of morning coffee now cold. Nicholas unfolded a small map of the city and studied it for the tenth time. "Bridges all over the place," he said.

"But of course," said Tewksbury. "'Bruges' is the Flemish word for 'bridges,' after all. It's a very old city, probably founded about A.D. 700. In those days the river Zwyn ran clear to the sea, and Bruges was a major port; the Venice of the North, they called it. But by 1490 the river had silted up, and the ships stopped coming. For Bruges, time stopped in 1490."

"And where do we find Caspar?"

"We're here," said the old man, touching a point of the little map. "There's the cathedral and the main square, as you can see. Caspar Van der Ek is here," he said, moving his finger a bit, "across the square on the first street behind the ring road. A ten-minute walk, no more." He paused. "Number 66."

"Right," said Nicholas. "I've got the drawings. Let's go."

Number 66 bore no sign. It was a drab storefront with a door and a grimed display window just wide enough to hold one truly hideous green plastic armchair, billious with accumulated dust. Bits of fabric and a rusted hammer head lay on its seat.

"It pays to advertise," said Wren in a hollow voice. *"Look* at that monstrosity. I wouldn't give it to an enemy."

"Still there," murmured the old man, "after all these years. Very cunning man, our Caspar. It keeps people away, don't you see? It's better than a barred and locked door; yet it's a perfect cover. Precisely the way Caspar wants it. May I?" He turned the doorknob and walked in, Nicholas and Wren following. The shop was quite empty. Twelve feet or so back from the front door, a brick wall ran across the width of the room, broken by a black metal door.

Nicholas twisted the knob. "Locked," he said. He raised his hand to knock.

"Ah, three times, Nicholas. Then twice," said the professor softly. "Unless he's changed it after all these years."

Nicholas complied. There was a short pause. They heard

a bolt slide away, then another. The door inched open a slit. Nicholas came close and peered into a single magnified eye that studied him from behind a very thick lens.

"You are a tourist?" The voice was heavily accented, with a furry softness, something like a menacing stage whisper.

"No, sir."

"You have something to sell? We are not buying something now. Season finish."

"Uh, we're not selling anything, either."

"You wish to buy? Only one chair for sale. In front of my store. Nine hundred dollars. You want?"

"No, we're not buying anything, either. Look, Mr. Van der Ek, what we want is to talk—"

A chain rattled suddenly, and the door swung open a bit wider. Nicholas saw an extremely powerful hand shoot out to clamp his forearm so strongly that he winced. *"How do you know that name?"* the voice hissed. *"Who send you? Who are you?"*

"Good morning, Caspar," said Professor Tewksbury calmly. "Will you come out, or shall we come in? It's been a long time."

Slowly the door swung open, to reveal a chunky little muskrat of a man. He wore a long-sleeved woolen undershirt, open at the collar and tucked into a pair of stained black trousers. His head was thrust forward, and his back curved in a stoop that made him look almost hunchbacked. He was pasty pale in color, with a fringe of gray hair that bushed out at his temples. He squinted, studying the old professor's face with painful concentration.

"So! You again. This is how the young man knows how to knock on my door. I see . . . and I do not see. They are with you, Lewis Tewksbury?"

"They are with me, Caspar Van der Ek. We are here to talk with you for a bit. Shall we do it out here?"

The little man backed quickly through the black doorway. "Great god, what am I thinking of! Come in, all of you. *Vite, vite!*"

Behind the brick wall the room stretched forty to fifty feet deep. It was filled with chairs, end tables, lounges, vanities, sofas, tall breakfront cabinets—all illuminated by a single naked bulb that hung from the dead center of the room, casting a dyspeptic glare that dissolved and was lost in corner shadows.

The cabinetmaker shuffled through the maze to a walled office at the rear. He flicked a desk lamp on and settled into a chair, rubbing his pale fingers nervously over his bald pate.

"You bring more trouble, Lewis Tewksbury, yes? Then I warn you this time. I have strong friends now. So what?"

"No trouble this time, Caspar. Far, far from it. I'm not in that line of work anymore."

The cabinetmaker absorbed this in silence. He sat in the chair slumped over the desk, his pudgy hands palms down and slightly cupped. After a moment he lifted his eyes to study the professor's face. "You are not in that line of work anymore," he repeated.

"No," said the old man blandly. "In point of fact, I'm here as a . . . um . . . customer. I want to buy something."

"You want to buy something."

"I want to buy something. Something rather . . . ah . . . rather special."

"Something . . . rather special," repeated Van der Ek.

Tewksbury laughed. "We'll never get to it if you simply repeat everything I say, Caspar. My friends here and I have come to you from the United States with a commission. And a great deal of money for you. Do you want to know how much money, Caspar?"

Caspar remained silent. He turned first to Wren and studied her carefully. She smiled weakly. Then he swung his glance to Nicholas. "Who are these young people," he said, "these friends of yours who come from the United States?"

"All in good time, my friend. For the moment, let us say that this is Mr. and Mrs. . . . er . . . Bird."

The cabinetmaker nodded slowly at this transparent bit of misinformation. It was, Nicholas thought, as though he had expected just such a reply, and in some obscure way it reassured him.

"Mr. and Mrs. Bird," said Caspar. "You have such a nice name. How *much* money?" he said to Tewksbury.

"Ten thousand dollars, Caspar. United States dollars, my friend."

"As you say, Lewis Tewksbury, a great deal of money. And all for a little furniture store on a little street in a little town in Belgium. I have nothing for ten thousand dollars to sell you, Lewis Tewksbury. I say this with much regret, you understand?"

"Not quite," said the professor, with an edge of impatience in his tone. "We come across an ocean to the very best cabinetmaker in the world, to the greatest master craftsman now living, not to buy the foolish articles sold to greedy dealers, but to buy a supreme masterpiece!"

Van der Ek nodded. "So. It is to build something for you, then?"

Tewksbury nodded. "It is to build something for us, Caspar." The old man tilted his head to Nicholas. "Show him the drawings," he murmured.

"Right," said Nicholas. He opened the briefcase and pulled out the set of Riesener's drawings copied from the originals in the archives in Paris the week before. Wordlessly, he slid them to Caspar Van der Ek.

Their effect was electric. The cabinetmaker stiffened in his chair, then flipped his eyeglasses to the top of his head and bent forward, his nose inches from the surface of the paper. He mumbled excitedly to himself in Flemish, flipping the pages from detail to detail. The minutes went by. With a long sigh he settled back at last, shaking his head from side to side.

"I need to see what the old masters could do, to remind me of how much I must still learn," he said quietly. "You are here to have me build you a *bureau du roi* something like this beautiful thing here? Is so?"

Tewksbury shook his head. "Not something like it, Caspar. *Exactly* like it."

"So." Caspar winked slowly. "So," he repeated. "A copy. This is what you want Caspar Van der Ek to build?"

"For ten thousand dollars, my friend."

The cabinetmaker spread his hands. "But this is not honest, Lewis Tewksbury. A good copy can be made for a thousand dollars. Fifteen hundred dollars at the most. If you pay ten thousand dollars, then the rest is for my silence. I am very sorry. It cannot be done."

"Of course," said Tewksbury suavely, "there will have to be decoration of true gold, Caspar. That will cost more, and we are prepared to pay more. About five thousand more, I should say."

Caspar shook his head again. "You mean to commission a *true* copy, Lewis Tewksbury?"

"In every way, my friend. Perfect mother-of-pearl, perfect ebony, perfect tortoise, true glues, true varnishes—a true work of art in every detail!"

The little cabinetmaker sighed. "To make a true work of art for once," he whispered. "To prepare a piece as the masters did, with no compromise, no foolish tricks to cut the cost here and cut the cost there." He patted his fingertips together nervously. "It would be such a pleasure to me, to prove to myself what *asses* these experts are. *Just for once!*"

He shook his head mournfully. "I am sorry. There are

two very big reasons why I cannot help you, Lewis Tewksbury. The money is not enough. It must be more. Much
more."

"And the other reason," said Tewksbury placidly.

"It is against the law to sell such a copy, unless you tell
the buyer it *is* a copy. I do not think this is what you
and . . . and your friends plan to do. I am sorry. For ten
thousand dollars? No. The risk is too much."

"How much, Caspar?" said Tewksbury softly.

"Fifty thousand dollars," said Caspar.

"Oh, dear me, no," said the professor. "Out of the question. We hadn't planned to go to Spain, Caspar. Nevertheless, Antonio Villela of Córdoba is almost your equal as a
master. We'd have much preferred to give our commission
to you. But fifty thousand dollars! I'm very sorry, my friend.
We'd best go now."

"Villela!" The pudgy little man seemed to spit the name.
"You rank *him* close to *me*? I did not think you so foolish."
He pulled at his lower lip. "True gold for the fittings? Ebony
and mother-of-pearl and tortoise from the very period? No
compromises?"

"None, Caspar."

The Belgian sighed again. "It is my opportunity. Why
should we quarrel? I will do it for forty thousand dollars."

"Ten."

"Thirty-five! See? I bend. Can you not bend a little, too?"

"Very well. I bend a little. Fifteen."

"Thirty."

"Twenty."

"*Twenty?* Do you know the work I must put aside? Do
you know the time this masterpiece demands? We cannot
put a price on such art, Lewis Tewksbury!"

"I agree," said the old man. "We will haggle no more.
You want thirty. I will pay twenty. We will settle in the mid-
dle—for twenty-five thousand. Done."

"Done," said Casper. He rubbed his hands together slowly, like a surgeon washing up. "Twenty-five thousand dollars—with five more for the gold."

"And Mr. Bird here will tell you about the . . . special modifications we'll need."

Caspar swung on Nicholas. "There are to be no compromises," he said coldly. "It is the agreement."

Nicholas nodded. "I know. But Riesener was famous for his secret compartments and concealed locks. They were his mark. We'll need two."

The cabinetmaker nodded. "Yes, young man, these are not compromises. But I find no drawings for these in the papers. Where are they to be?"

"We think you are Riesener's equal as a master," said Nicholas. "We can tell you where he placed them in four other tables. And how he concealed them. But we thought you should design these yourself."

Van der Ek turned to the professor. "Your young man has more in him than the eye sees. I like much the sound of what he says. Very well. I will create two secret compartments. When I am finished, you will look for them. I will challenge you to find them, Lewis Tewksbury. Yes, even you."

"Twenty-five thousand, Caspar," said the professor, "whether I find them or not. But they must be large enough to hold some papers and jewelry."

"I understand, Lewis Tewksbury. Papers and jewelry. For your provenance, eh? Nice. Very, very nice. It is a splendid thing you do. But I am troubled, honored professor. You come to me because you know what I do. I make copies. Once you stood with the law and the good experts. Now you plan this grand forgery. You pay so much money. Is it permitted to know why you have changed . . . sides?"

Tewksbury stood up unexpectedly and walked to the

door. He peered into the gloom of the room beyond and spoke softly. "My life was teaching, my university, my books, Caspar. They said I was too old. Finished. They forced me to retire. Go away and die, old man. That's what they were thinking. You are no longer of any use to us—or to anybody." He turned and lifted his hands. "I tried it, Caspar. For nine years I tried it. Watering the damn rubber plants. Cleaning their leaves, one by one. Shopping for my eggs and bread and butter and tea. And hearing the clock *ticking my life away.* I *am* old, Caspar. But not inside. Inside, I'm quick. I'm full of life. You understand?"

Caspar sighed. "I will be seventy soon, Lewis Tewksbury. Of course I know what you say. Always, I could say to myself, 'Caspar, you are a lucky man. You have as many years ahead of you as you have behind you. Long years, good years ahead.' Always, it made me feel good. But when a man is 70, he does not say this anymore. You want to do something *grand,* just as I do. Isn't it?"

"That's it, my friend."

"Very good. This I now begin to see. But *these* young people," he said, turning his chin toward Nicholas and Wren briefly. "Where do they enter the scene? This I do *not* see."

"Why," said Tewksbury, smiling, "the whole idea is from the lively brain of our Mr. Bird here. As you say, there is more to him than meets the eye. As for . . . um . . . Mrs. Bird, she is a lady bountiful of considerable resources."

"The money," said Caspar, "comes from Mrs. Bird. *Alors!* You are a collection of most improbable criminals, the three of you."

"Yes," said Nicholas, "we're counting on that to help us. *And* your silence, Mr. Van der Ek."

"And my silence, as you say. You must not fear that I talk to somebody."

For the first time, Wren spoke. "Strong friends," she said. "You told the professor that you had some new friends. Very strong, you said they were. Who?"

Nicholas and the professor exchanged a startled glance. Only Wren had remembered the soft threat from Caspar and had thought about it.

"I'd quite forgotten that, Caspar," said Tewksbury. "Who *are* these new friends of yours?"

"You have been away from the world markets," mumbled Caspar. He seemed, suddenly, deflated and tense. "It is best that you do not ask this question and that I do not answer it."

"No, sir. Not possible," said Wren gently. "There's no way we can be a little big pregnant. We work together—or we don't. No partway partnership. Won't work. We *have* to know."

"I feared you would say so," said Caspar. "But why do you not believe me! I say I stay silent. I stay. I say it is best that you do not know. It is best!"

"I agree with Mrs. Bird," said Nicholas. "You had better tell us."

"I'm afraid so, Caspar. We will not walk blind into some sort of trouble. Either you tell us, or we pack up and pay a call on Villela."

"But . . . but Villela will say nothing," grated the Belgian. "Villela also, he works for him."

"Who is *him?*" said Wren.

"Roland Swain." The cabinetmaker groaned softly. "That devil Roland Swain. That is *him!*"

Nine

To those who love her, London remains the queen among the cities of the world. But love is blind about cities too, and London chokes with her traffic and reeks of her traffic fumes. She is noisy and often dirty and as the New Yorkers say, it's a nice place to visit, period.

Yet even in London there is relief to be found, if one is rich enough. Eaton Square is lovely, and so is Belgravia. And if one is very rich, there is always Rutland Gate. It hides behind old walls of stone, very near to Harrods and the green lawns of Hyde Park. Behind the walls the cobbled lanes are narrow and tree-lined; the sounds of London seem mute and murmurous. It may cost the earth, as Londoners say, but it is surely worth it.

At 65-A, on Rutland Court Road, Mr. Roland Swain slipped a solid-gold key into the lock and pushed the heavy oaken door open. Reaching inside, he carefully flipped the switch that disconnected his private system of alarms, wiped his feet fastidiously on the monogrammed mat, and entered.

He was a very little man, almost jockey size, no more than five feet tall. He carried himself most erect, as smallish men seem always to do, but primly—like the tactful rector of a wealthy church. His mild blue eyes looked out at the world benevolently, and Mr. Swain would have been genuinely shocked to hear himself described, as Caspar had indeed described him, as a devil.

Not at all, he would have thought. He wouldn't have said it aloud, however, for he spoke as little as possible. But he would not have agreed. Roland Swain knew himself to be, above all else in this world, a man of common sense. Common sense had made him powerful and rich. Common sense had led him to enter divinity school as a young man without independent means. The Church was rich; it took care of its own, didn't it? But common sense soon taught him that it was men of wealth who *made* the Church rich. Who were these men of wealth? Those who sold things and took money *in* were always richer than those who bought things and paid money *out*. But of course. How obvious, how logical. Inevitably, common sense confronted doctrine.

"There are nearly two hundred churches in Europe who say they possess one of the nails of the true cross," he had said long ago, to one of his instructors. "How can this be?"

"The Roman Catholics have records on such things in Rome, Mr. Swain. Here, we are Anglicans, with more important questions to ask."

"And there are nearly fifty churches—forty-six, I think—who say they own one of Saint Peter's fingers. Very puzzling, sir."

"They may slice one finger into forty-six bits, Mr. Swain. But really—"

"There are also several hundred churches, mostly in Spain, who have spent their wealth to buy a bit of Christ's own robe. What about *that*, sir?"

The instructor had dismissed him irritatedly and written a chilly letter to his bishop. In due course Roland Swain was advised to reconsider his calling, to face up to the unhappy fact that he was not quite suited to do God's work on earth. It was suggested that he resign. And so he did. Roland Swain had plans.

In the following year he sold seven very old and very rusted nails and four bits of nondescript woolen cloth. The forged documents attesting to the authenticity of these impressive relics he produced himself, dipping sheets of parchment paper into weak tea and composing the Latin texts with scrupulous care. The small ivory cases to hold these treasures had cost him five pounds each. He went to Spain in his religious habit, pausing briefly at Madrid, Seville, Toledo, Barcelona, Avila, and Valladolid. He spoke his uncertain Spanish softly, told his story simply, and brought back almost five thousand pounds as clear profit. Those who sold things took money *in*. The demand was great, the supply small. Common sense.

That was how it had started, some forty years ago. Roland Swain worked hard, worked cautiously and prospered. After that first foray into Spain, however, he saw the need for organization. Artists to produce pictures, wood-carvers to produce church art, potters and glaziers, silversmiths and printers. Little by little, he established his network. Now, in ten cities in Spain, agents worked to his orders. There were seven more in Italy, five in France, two in Belgium, two in Portugal, two in West Germany, one in East Germany, four in Egypt, four in Greece, two in Turkey, three in Mexico, one in Russia, five in Japan—forty-eight in all.

For Roland Swain they bought and sold, found craftsmen to produce things collectors and dealers wanted, forged the documents, collected the money, keeping their agreed share. They were utterly reliable, utterly loyal to their master.

Because if they were not, Roland Swain would call upon Alexander Peel, and Alexander Peel would have them killed. Or blinded. Or maimed.

It was only common sense. No Turk will remain loyal forever. No Italian continues to be reliable. It is against their very natures, Swain knew. But if one lets it be known to a Turkish metalworker that his treason will cause his arms to be severed at the elbows, that Turk remains loyal.

Still, Roland Swain paid his people well. Not too much, but not too little; it was an important element of his power. To put any man under the threat of such frightening punishment made a judicious policy of reward essential. And so it was that year by year the network grew and Roland Swain grew richer with it.

Now he hung his black topcoat in the closet, placed his bowler on the shelf above it, and climbed up the graceful stairway to the floor above. An open fire burned quietly in the grate to the right, and the late-afternoon sunlight filtered through the patterned curtains, giving the room a gentle glow. He walked to his desk at the window and lifted the phone, depressing one of the four buttons at its base. A tape-recorded voice spoke metallically.

"Cairo called at two-thirty."

He pressed the second button.

"Brussels called at two-forty-five."

There were no other messages.

Cairo, he thought. That would be Hassam. He employed

several families in a tiny village near Medinet Habu. The mortuary temples of Ramses II were nearby, and the whole area was a mine of Egyptian antiquities. It was also true that the clay of the adjacent banks of the Nile could be baked into delectable little copies of predynastic gods and goddesses—cat gods and falcon gods and serpent gods made by the villagers to Hassam's order, by the thousands. Tourists loved them, and the dealers' demands grew with every passing year. The clay was cheap enough, thought Swain wryly. A very healthy part of the enterprise. Was something amiss? Hassam tended to be excitable, like most Egyptians.

Brussels? That might be more troublesome. Planchet was the soul of prudence, and rarely called. His network of artisans produced the Dürer copies, the fake medieval laces, fake church art, and fake French furniture, with surpassing skill and very high profits. If Planchet called, it had to be important. He dialed the familiar number.

"Good afternoon," the voice said. "Peel's Flower Shop. Who is calling, please?"

"Good afternoon, Peel. Roger Swain here. I'll be needing some flowers, I think."

"Happy to serve you, as always, Mr. Swain. Anything special in mind, sir?"

"Roses, I think, Peel."

"Then I'll suggest tea roses, sir. Lovely shipment came in, just fresh this afternoon. Yellow, sir. Will they do?"

"Splendid, Peel. Yellow it is. How many, do you think?"

"Two dozen, I should say, sir. You'll need two dozen for a proper centerpiece."

"As many as that? Very well, Peel. Two dozen. You'll send them along?"

"In half an hour, sir. I'll bring them myself."

"Why, thank you, Peel. Very good of you."

"Always like to take care of our better customers myself, Mr. Swain."

"Half an hour, then. Good-bye, Peel."

Roland Swain replaced the phone thoughtfully. Tea roses; that would be Bruges. Yellow—Caspar Van der Ek. But *twenty-four?* Peel killed on any code number over *twelve.* Old Caspar Van der Ek?

What was going on in Bruges?

"My god," said Wren, rubbing the palm of her hand across her eyes. "This is unbelievable. You mean there's this sort of mastermind who controls the world markets for fake art and fake antiques? I mean, are you *sure* about this?"

"I am sure."

"What's he like? I mean, is he a killer?"

Caspar shook his head slightly. "I never see him, I never talk to him. Only Planchet. Him I see."

"Who the hell is Planchet?"

"My cousin. He lives in Brussels. Twice a year he come to Bruges with my money and my new work. *He* tell me about Roland Swain."

"And you say it's dangerous for you to go off on your own and do work for us, is that right?" said Nicholas.

"Planchet has warned me. I must work only for Roland Swain. It would go very bad for me if I disobeyed." The cabinetmaker shrugged.

"But, then, why did you agree to do our table?" said Wren. "Aren't you afraid?"

"From Planchet I take five thousand dollars in your American money every year. In Bruges, it is enough. But also it keeps me here. You are American. I think you cannot understand. With your twenty-five thousand dollars, I can leave."

"Leave?" said Wren blankly. "Where will you go?"

"Why," said Caspar softly, "to America. Two hundred million people. Think of it! Not even Roland Swain will find me!" He looked at Professor Tewksbury and nodded again. "You, I think, will understand. I wish to be *free*."

"Well, then," said the professor, "we'll have to make sure that Roland Swain doesn't find out about this little project, hmm?"

Those who spend their time working as officers of the law soon discover that nobody ever *looks* like a criminal. Victims, confronted by the man who has robbed them, are always shocked. "Why," they say, "he looks just like an ordinary person!" It is, alas, too often true that the most successful criminals tend to resemble somebody's favorite uncle. Alexander Peel, who had people killed, or who killed them himself, filled these specifications to the letter.

He parked his trim little van precisely along the tradesmen's curb. He carried the box of flowers carefully in his left hand, ringing the rear-door bell just once, and briefly. When Swain's butler came to the door, Peel lifted his hat politely.

"Good afternoon, Mr. Hodd," said Alexander Peel.

"Good afternoon, Peel," said the butler. "Mr. Swain is expecting you. You are to go right on up to the front room."

"Thank you very much, Mr. Hodd. Thank you very much indeed."

Smiling, Peel moved through the kitchen toward the stairwell that led to the floor above. He was about forty, of middling height, with bright brown eyes and reddish-brown hair that grew close to his skull in tight little curls. His skin was very white and faintly freckled. As he moved, he seemed to make hardly a sound, and even as Hodd listened, he could not hear Peel's foot upon the stair.

Mr. Hodd did not like Alexander Peel. Why, he could

not say. There was something about the man that made him uneasy. He seemed to be a favorite of Mr. Swain, which was also a bit odd. For, as the butler knew, Mr. Swain rarely entertained and had no favorites. Yet, here was Peel again, with his flowers. Four or five times a year he would come, and Mr. Swain always saw him privately. Well, Mr. Swain was a gentleman, and the affairs of gentlemen were no concern of his. Hodd turned his attention back to the daily newspaper and, as always, forgot about Peel at once.

Thus he exploded the myth that no man can keep a secret from his butler. Hodd served Mr. Swain well and would have sworn an oath in any court that his master was a respectable man of independent means who invested in stocks and bonds. Mr. Swain a criminal? His hand on the Holy Bible itself, Hodd would have sworn again that the idea was monstrous and quite impossible.

"You spoke to Planchet yourself, Peel?"

"Indeed I did, Mr. Swain. He was very definite, if I may say so. Described all three of them."

"And Planchet's informant?"

"An old widow who lives across the way. Barrault, her name is. Planchet has paid her for years, just to report who goes in and out of Van der Ek's shop. She called straightaway, Planchet says."

"Yes. A wise policy. It has proved itself many times, hasn't it, Peel?"

"Indeed it has, sir."

"Very well. Who are they, then?"

"Two young people. They seem to be Americans. A young man and a young woman—in their twenties, the Barrault woman thought. And quite a nice-looking young couple, too, she says."

"Come on, man. You're sitting on your egg too long. Hatch it out, Peel."

"Let me tell you, Mr. Swain, it's a fair shocker. These two young visitors had one of Caspar's old friends along to keep them company. You'll remember him, sir, from some years back. Tall, the Barrault woman said, with white hair and nice wrinkles on his face. Thin, he was, with a little black walking stick. And very old, of course."

"Tewksbury!" said Roland Swan. "Lewis Tewksbury and his walking stick! As you say, Peel, a fair shocker indeed." ·

"And Caspar Van der Ek knows quite a bit more now than he knew when Tewksbury meddled into your affairs last time, sir. It felt like . . . like a right proper emergency to me, Mr. Swain."

"You've done the right thing, of course, Peel. But we'll move carefully, as ever. You will call Planchet tonight, please. I want Tewksbury followed. He called the police once. We'll not be surprised *this* time. Watch those two young people, as well. I want to know their movements. Who they see, where they go. The usual drill, Peel. Planchet is to stay away from Van der Ek. They're related, you know. Convey to Pierre my grateful thanks for this evidence of his loyalty. Lay it on a bit, Peel. But I repeat, he is not to communicate with Caspar Van der Ek under any circumstances. You may put a bit of steel into your tone on that one, I think. Planchet will want to know what will happen to Caspar. Reassure him, Peel. Tell him that Caspar is one of our most valued suppliers and that his record over the years has been immaculate. That will do for now, I think."

"You'll be wanting your reports, sir. How often?"

"Daily, Peel, daily. Tewksbury may be on to something with our loyal supplier Van der Ek. I want to know what it is. I'll call you at five o'clock or so."

"Five it is, sir. Will that be all?"

Roland Swain stared up into Peel's bright brown eyes and nodded benignly. "I think so, Peel." The little man flicked a bit of dust from the surface of his desk. "For the present," he murmured.

Peel's eyes gleamed for the barest moment. "Then I'll be taking my leave, sir. I'll see myself out. Shall I have Hodd fix your tea roses?"

"Do that, Peel, please. You're most helpful."

"I try to be, sir."

Roland Swain could not hear him as he went downstairs.

Ten

They met, as usual, in the lobby of the Portinari for their morning coffee.

"About ten thousand dollars should do, Miss Wooding. You might bring twelve or fourteen, just to be on the safe side." Tewksbury's voice was serene.

"Let me do this one more time, professor," said Wren, her voice taut. "Two good emeralds, small. Two good rubies, also small. Twenty or thirty small pink pearls, loose. Not strung. A dozen or so small white diamonds, very fine. Is that it? Won't I stick out like a flagpole, buying all this stuff?"

"You go to three or four dealers," said Nicholas patiently. "Amsterdam has been selling precious stones for centuries. You're just one more rich kid shopping for jewels in the gemstone capital of the world. Don't sweat it. No one will even notice you."

"Dutch. I don't talk Dutch. I can barely listen to it—all full of clicks and clacks. What about *that?*"

"Every dealer you'll meet will speak half a dozen languages, my dear," said Tewksbury. "Or more. It's one of the tools of their trade. No, I agree with Nicholas. You'll be just fine."

Wren shrugged. "I'll be just fine. Right. I fly to Amsterdam tomorrow. From the airport I take a cab to the Krasnapolsky Hotel. I don't check in, but I make like a guest. I ask the clerk: 'Please, sir, who are some of the big diamond and jewel dealers, and where are they located, because I want to buy some nice jewels for my mother.'"

"Unset gems, Wren. No rings, no brooches. Just the stones," said Nicholas.

"Got it. Unset and unsettled. Like me."

"It's important, Wren."

"I know, I know. So I go to three or four places, pay the cash, and get the hell back to the airport. Fly to Brussels, bus to Bruges, bed. That it?"

"Perfect."

"How do I know they won't cheat me?" said Wren. "If you want to know why I'm so damn tense, that's why. Jezuzz! I don't know a good emerald from a hunk of bottle glass. Shouldn't we get an expert to do this for us?"

"In this case, no, my dear," said Tewksbury. "The gem dealers of Amsterdam have a long and distinguished history for scrupulous integrity. It's one of the reasons why they've made their city the center of the trade. You're young, American, and most attractive, if I may say so. The dealers will doubtless work very hard to give you full value. No doubt about it."

"Clarity," mumbled Wren, "and no flaws. Square cuts. No tinge of yellow in the diamonds. No modern cuts. Pinkish pearls." She shook her head. "All of a sudden I'm a big gem buyer."

A French Finish

"The stones and the pearls will help us to win friends and influence people, my dear. It's just the sort of touch that helps to establish authenticity. Marie Antoinette would have the gems ready to be set into a tiny frame of a painted miniature, a sort of keepsake for her royal lover. What is more natural than to hide them in the new desk?"

"I know, I know. Right. I'm off. The bus to Brussels leaves in two hours or so. I'll get the cash out of the hotel safe and go up to my room to pack a bag and freshen up." She tilted her head at Nicholas. "You want to help, Admiral?"

"You get the cash and go on up. I'll be along in a few minutes," said Nicholas. He smiled. "I'll help," he murmured.

She colored faintly and stole a glance at the old man. He seemed to be fascinated with the button on the cuff of his shirt. They watched her walk from the lounge toward the desk.

"You're off to Paris, Nicholas?"

"I am, sir. I'll go to Brussels on the midnight bus and fly to Orly tomorrow. Ebony, mother-of-pearl, and tortoiseshell. In those big old jewelry boxes, as you said."

"Quite right. You'll find that dozens of dealers sell them. The supply is certain to be plentiful. I think you might buy one or two ivory boxes as well, if you can find them. Ivory will make an attractive variation in the inlay. Quite in keeping with Oeben's style, too."

"Ivory. Will do. And you're off for London?"

"Tomorrow morning, bright and early. The gold market in London will serve our needs perfectly. It's about a hundred and thirty dollars an ounce at the moment. Two pounds should do us nicely. I'll bring it straight back."

"That's it, then." Nicholas rose and stretched. "I'll go on up. I want to say good-bye to Wren. She's a bit nervous."

Surprisingly, Tewksbury winked.

* * *

The bed was turned down. Wren lay on her back staring at the ceiling, her arms behind her head. There was a knock at the door.

"It's not locked," she called.

"You're all *dressed*," said Nicholas, his voice mildly outraged. "Damnit, Wren, I want to make love, and we haven't too much time."

"I ought to be courted more," said Wren. "That's the whole trouble with this relationship. Bang, bang, Wren is ready. Bang, bang, Wren is banged. Bang, bang, Wren is off and running to buy some pretty stones. If *that's* romance, you can have my share."

"It's true," said Nicholas. "On the other hand, it's mostly your doing."

"*My* doing?" Wren pulled herself up to one elbow. "When did I ever tell you I didn't want a love poem? When did I say I didn't care to hear sweet nothings whispered into my ear?"

"You've been the more aggressive, Wren, now admit it." Nicholas grinned. "Roses are red, violets are blue. Get undressed 'cause I love you."

"That's *terrible*," said Wren. But she seemed more cheerful. "It's true. I have been more aggressive. Why, do you think?"

Nicholas turned the lock on the door and came over to sit beside her. He slipped open the first button of her blouse very slowly, and the next, then leaned forward and kissed her very softly on the chest.

"Hey," said Wren, "that's nice. You never did that before."

He leaned up to whisper into her ear, and she blushed a very bright red.

"Wow. I never tried *that*. Really?"

"It's what Ovid called one of those sweet nothings you whisper in the ear of your ladylove."

"Ovid, huh? Can I help you with the buttons?"

"No, Wren. You're teaching me to be more aggressive. I think I like it."

"You sure this is going to work?"

"They knew about it five thousand years ago. It'll work."

"No wonder they called it the Golden Age of Greece," said Wren.

"Peel?"

"Good afternoon, sir. It's been a busy day."

"The old man?"

"On his way to London, sir."

"*Here?* You're quite sure?"

"No doubt about it, sir. Planchet's man is right in the hotel. Saw him pick up his tickets."

"You're having him . . . ah . . . followed?"

"That we are, sir. Busset."

"And the other two?"

"Well, now, that's very interesting, sir. The young man is off to Paris, and the young lady is in Amsterdam at this very moment. What with everything, Planchet wasn't able to have them followed as well. We weren't ready with enough of our own people to follow them all. Planchet called me, and I told him to keep Busset on the old man's trail." There was a small silence. "I do hope I did the right thing, sir," said Peel, faint worry in his voice.

"I hope so, Peel. I'd like to know just where the old man settles, once he's here in London. You may call me on this private line, Peel."

"That I will, sir, just as soon as I hear."

"And, Peel? There's one more thing."

"Yes, sir?"

"Let's take this opportunity to see if we can't put some sort of listening device into their rooms at the hotel in Bruges, shall we? And a tap on their telephones, if it can be arranged? And what about Mr. Van der Ek's premises—do we have them covered with some sort of electronic surveillance?"

"I'm not sure, sir. I'll speak to Planchet at once. May I take it that you are concerned about our friend Caspar, sir?"

"I suppose so, Peel. In any case, I want him covered. I think I begin to see the outlines of a very large amount of money behind all this extraordinary activity. We'll continue to walk very softly for a bit, Peel, and see what we can learn. There may be profit in it."

"Very good, sir. Walk softly it shall be."

Professor Tewksbury completed his third stroll around Piccadilly Circus. In the reflection of a tobacconist's shop window he found the man again. Short, tweed coat, dark cap, dark hair, old briefcase; *still there.*

He had noticed the man shortly after leaving Brown's Hotel, not an hour earlier. Not because the man was particularly noticeable, of course. Tewksbury walked slowly toward him, smiling easily.

"Do you know Rowley's restaurant, by any chance? Right near here, on Jermyn Street? I'd like a cup of tea and a few sweet cakes. Will you join me?"

The man stared at him suspiciously and said nothing.

"Look, my friend," said the professor, "I've watched you watching me. Now, *really.* We're both grown men, too old for this sort of thing. Let's have a cup of tea, and I'll see if I can tell you what you want to know, and you can make your report. I'm too old to give you any trouble. What d'you say?"

The man studied Tewksbury's guileless face carefully

and heaved a sigh. His accent, heavily French, was quite cultured.

"I tell . . . I tell the man from Brussels that . . . that I do not do this sort of work. I am teacher."

"*Are* you? So am I! *Moi aussi! Comprenez?* Lewis Tewksbury, at your service."

"Busset. Albert Busset." The man bowed slightly, with a sort of sober dignity.

"So nice to make your acquaintance, Mr. Busset. *"C'est un plaisir de faire vôtre connaissance, monsieur!* What d'you say, then? *Café! Ou . . . du thé, peut-être?"*

"Tea, yes," said Busset. "You are most kind."

"You'll like Rowley's. It's just down the street here, and around the corner. Quiet, with excellent service, and we can have our little talk."

It took no more than ten minutes of such amiable chatter to convince Albert Busset that the aged Professeur Tewksbury was no more dangerous than a garden butterfly. The tea was piping hot. The little pastries were delicious. The restaurant was clean and quiet. Busset dropped some of his Gallic reserve.

"I know less about this than you do," he said moodily. "That is the truth of it. I am to follow you. From Bruges, to here. I do it. I am to say where you go; to what hotel, you understand? I do it. Then, I am to see what else you do; who you meet and so on and on."

"Fair enough," said Tewksbury suavely. "If you've followed me from Bruges, you know I've come from Caspar. Since you know Caspar, you know his cousin, eh? And as for London, you know I'm at Brown's Hotel. I'm going to buy something rather expensive here, Mr. Busset. I *can* tell you that much."

"But you cannot say to me what it is?" said Busset.

"I'm afraid not. Unless, of course, you care to make a sort of . . . of trade. An *exchange,* so to speak."

Busset sipped his tea and gave the appearance of much thought. "Alas, I cannot think of what I might tell you. Already you know what I know, Mr. Tewksbury."

"Not quite," said the old man very gently. "You might know who Planchet reports to. I'd like to know that name. Tell me that, and I'll tell you what I'm here to buy. That is the exchange I had in mind."

"Tempting," said Busset bleakly. "Also very *dangereux*, I regret to say. No, Mr. Tewksbury. I must decline. I do not have the very happy life, but it is the only life I possess, and I want very much to keep it. Let us enjoy our tea and say no more about this 'exchange,' please."

"We'll consider the matter closed," murmured the old man placidly. "Do try one of these little pink things. I think you'll like them."

"Swain here."

"Peel, sir. Busset called Planchet an hour ago, and Planchet called me a few minutes ago. Our friend Tewksbury is at Brown's Hotel."

"*Ex*-cellent, Peel. Well done."

"There's more, sir. Tewksbury spotted our man Busset and invited him to tea and cakes at Rowley's!"

"You're joking."

"Dead serious I am, sir. He offered to tell Busset what he was going to buy here, if Busset gave him my name."

"And . . . ?"

"Busset thought it best not to."

"Very wise of our Mr. Busset."

"My thought exactly, sir."

"And Tewksbury gave no clue, no hint?"

"Only that it was something very expensive. He did say that. Busset was certain."

"Ahhhh." Roland Swain smiled contentedly. With Tewksbury, something substantial was afoot, after all.

Common sense. "Thank you, Peel. That will be all for now. You're to keep me informed, remember."

"That I will, sir."

Like a small spider, Roland Swain sat at his desk. The fly had touched the strand. Soon he must stir himself and be enmeshed. He touched the tip of his finger to the bell that summoned Hodd.

"I'll have dinner now, Hodd, if cook is ready." He rose and moved to the dining room down the hall. "I'm *quite* hungry, in fact."

Eleven

They gathered in the tiny office in the back of Caspar's shop. On his dusty desk, under the light, the gems from Amsterdam gleamed prettily. Ranged around them were stacks of little boxes—three of ebony, two of mother-of-pearl, and two of tortoise. A flat box of ivory rested at the center, next to a chunky little bar of solid gold.

"The gold fools you," said Wren, "but my god, is it ever heavy."

"Is it enough?" said Nicholas.

Caspar nodded. "For two drawer pulls, the gold flange around the keyhole, the tips for the legs, and the little guard frieze across the back and around the corners, yes. It will be more than enough." He gave Nicholas a keen glance. "You had no difficulty in Paris?"

"A piece of cake," murmured Nicholas. The cabinetmaker looked puzzled. "No difficulty at all, I mean. I found the eight boxes in less than three hours, and I was back at Orly airport an hour after that."

"Amsterdam was also this . . . piece of cake?" said Caspar.

"Easy as pie," said Wren, grinning. "If it's a piece of cake, it's as easy as pie, Mr. Van der Ek. In Amsterdam all the gemstones are sold along the Kalver-Straat. I had some trouble tracking down the pearls. One dealer told me to go to Istanbul; it's the pearl center. But I found some."

Caspar turned to the professor. "And all went well in London, Lewis Tewksbury?"

"I'm curious about the wood for your desk, my friend. Before I tell you about my visit to London, let's discuss that first, if you don't mind. Finding the proper wood might be a bit of a problem, you know."

"Of course, professor. The wood is the key to it all. It does not make the piece of cake because the wood is old, eh? It is the finish put down by those who make it long ago. You understand?"

"Not really," said Wren. "I thought old wood was old wood."

"But *no*," said Caspar emphatically. "So many of the collectors are fooled. They think only the new wood will shrink or crack or warp. But old wood is alive, young woman. Until it rots, it is alive. Yes, the sap dries. But it too can crack and warp without the finish. It is the varnish, the lac, the wax. These harden; they make the tough skin, the *patine*, as we say. You understand?"

"And it can't be faked?" asked Wren.

"Impossible."

"Nor," murmured Tewksbury, "dare we try. The imitation of true patina is one of the first things the experts will look for. As I say, a problem. More than I first realized."

"Where do we start to look for this wood?" said Nicholas.

"The wood I have been saving for many years," said Caspar smugly. He gave an impish grin and tapped a knuckle slowly on the surface of his disreputable desk. "Right here."

Wren stared at him. "You don't mean this thing, do you?" She bent down to study the surface more carefully. "It looks awful. What do you do? Sandpaper it?"

"It was the writing table," said Caspar proudly. "It is perhaps two hundred years old. I myself find it in a monastery near Blois. The finish is as Oeben and Riesener worked; a simple method, but much time and much skill. Sandpaper first, as you say. For them, sandstone. Then the shellac, not very much, to mix with the alcohol. Then, rub with the very soft cloth. It dry. More of the mixture. Again, rub. Dry, again. Always with the same cloth, many, many times, until the luster is exactly correct. Then, the linseed oil. At night, the wood rest. In the morning, again the linseed oil. This is the French finish. It cannot be copied. Soft to the touch, shining, very strong."

"I'm sorry," said Wren helplessly, "but I'm missing something." She fingered the surface lightly. "This looks like junk, and it feels like junk!"

"Not there," purred Caspar. "Feel *underneath*, please."

Nicholas, Wren, and the professor exchanged startled glances and reached down to feel the underside of Caspar's desk.

"Fantastic," breathed Wren. "It's like satin!"

"Exactly," said Caspar complacently.

Nicholas bent down to have a look. Underneath, tucked well back into the corner, and less than an inch from the top of his nose, his eyes focused on the black metal mesh of the tiniest of microphones. A thin wire, dullish gray, led down the leg of the desk to a pin-size hole in the floor.

"The wood is surprisingly thick," he said calmly. "Like my head." He rose, beckoning to Wren and the professor with a firm gesture. "We have to go now, Mr. Van der Ek." Something in his tone brought Wren's head up in mild surprise, but she rose at once and went to the door. Frowning ever so faintly, Tewksbury followed.

"I go to work," said Caspar. "Tomorrow. Remember to bring the money, yes?"

"There's a goddamn microphone stuck under Caspar's desk," said Nicholas. They were walking slowly across the great square that fronted the cathedral. Wren's hand flew to her mouth. The professor stopped in his tracks momentarily, lost in thought.

"Caspar put it there. I bet he did," said Wren. "He's *cunning,* remember? That's what you told us, professor. Caspar did it!"

"The hell he did," said Nicholas. "He's going to take that desk apart tomorrow. He said so. Why would he bug the same desk he's about to pull to pieces? Just to record this meeting? Doesn't make sense."

"There's one more thing," said Tewksbury. "I didn't want to tell Caspar about my trip to London, because I didn't want to worry him. I was followed, you know. By someone named Busset. He lives right here, in Bruges. Nicholas and I thought it best to say nothing about it."

"Not even to me? I'm in the gang."

"No need to worry you, my dear. It was my suggestion. Please do not be offended."

"And this Busset—what about him?"

"A nice little man. We had tea together."

Wren blinked.

"Yes, tea. I had some hope of persuading him to tell me who had put him on my trail."

"And did he?"

"No, my dear girl, he did not. But he did drop one name."

"Not Caspar?"

"No, not Caspar."

Wren thought hard. "Roland Swain, then!"

"No, it was Planchet who employed him, I'm quite sure."

They mounted the steps leading into the lobby of the hotel. Nicholas paused at the doorway. "It's complicated," he mumbled. "Caspar's office is bugged. So somebody wants to know what he's up to. Right. *We're* what he's up to, so we may be bugged, too. Our rooms, I mean."

"Right here in the hotel?" whispered Wren.

Tewksbury nodded. "The probability is high that Nicholas is quite right, I should say." He rubbed the side of his nose reflectively. "The telephones in our rooms may be tapped, you know. Or they may have a paid informer on the hotel staff." He looked at them from under his silvery white eyebrows. "It seems to me that the question is this: should we try to find these little microphones or try to uncover this informer, or should we use them to our own advantage?"

"By feeding a lot of phony talk to them. Right?" said Wren.

"Almost," said Nicholas. "I've been thinking about it. It's complicated, because it won't work *either* way. If we find the microphones or the informer, they'll just put in more microphones and more informers, and hide them better. And they'd know that *we* know. But if we feed a lot of fake talk into the damn things—like, say, we're here to do research or something—then we'd have to stay a million miles away from Caspar. But, see, they already know we've been there, so that's no good either. Another thing. Do we tell Caspar about his little microphone? He's all right, but he thinks he's *safe.* I think the first thing I've got to do is to go back there and get that goddamn microphone the hell out of Caspar's office. There's probably a tape recorder down in the basement, too. I saw the wire. It goes right down the leg of the desk and through the floor."

"What are you going to do," said Wren, "break in?"

"That's against the law," said Nicholas blandly. "No, the professor here is going to invite Caspar out to dinner. We're going to get him very drunk tonight. So drunk, we'll have to help him home. He lives on the floor over his shop, right? So we'll take him upstairs, and while you tuck him in, I'll borrow his keys and let myself in downstairs. I think it should work, *if* we do it right. It better."

"Tortoiseshell, mother-of-pearl, ivory, and ebony, you say, Peel?"

"Right, sir. And the bar of gold. Planchet picked up the tape no more than half an hour ago, put in a fresh spool, and called me. They're going to make a fake desk, Mr. Swain. Louis XVI, Planchet thinks. Those items are for the inlays and marquetry, he says."

"And the jewels?"

"Hard to say, sir. They came from Amsterdam—that's all the tape says."

"Odd. This sort of furniture was never decorated with precious jewels. I wonder what Tewksbury has up his sleeve?"

"Sir?"

"Never mind, Peel. What of the wood itself? Have they got the wood for the reproduction, do you know?"

"I've been saving that one, Mr. Swain. Very clever, that! It's Caspar's desk, sir! A very old piece of wood, according to what Planchet heard."

"Caspar's *desk?* You're sure?"

"Oh, yes, sir."

"And where was the microphone placed, Peel?"

"Usual place, sir. Underneath, tucked right up in the corner."

"Why, damnit, Peel, you're not thinking. Caspar will

very shortly take that same desk apart. I do not want him to find that microphone. You understand? Call Planchet at once, man. He is in Bruges, I take it?"

"That he is, Mr. Swain."

"Then call him at once. I'm not ready to deal with Caspar. Not quite yet. Tell Planchet to remove every bit of that equipment, and to do so tonight. Our friend Van der Ek should be well asleep by now, so see to it, Peel. See to it."

"He's like a bag of wet sand," whispered Wren.

The professor pointed the beam of the flashlight at the door to Caspar's flat. Nicholas propped Caspar against the wall, his palm firm on the little man's chest. Wren struggled to keep the besotted cabinetmaker from sagging.

"I've unlocked the door," said Nicholas. "You two get him undressed and into bed. I'm going to the basement. I'll need the flashlight, professor."

Caspar lifted his eyelids and discovered Wren. He smiled and swung tipsily from the wall, reaching to embrace her.

"*Mes petits oiseaux,*" he crooned softly, "*baisez-moi, je vous en prie!*"

"What the hell is that all about?" said Wren.

"You're his little birds." Tewksbury grinned. "He must see two or three of you. He wants a kiss. It might be advisable, my dear. On the cheek, of course."

Nicholas watched them for a moment as they steered Caspar through the open door, then moved silently down the stairs. The entry hall below ran the full depth of the house, and Nicholas turned away from the front door and walked back along the narrow hall to the stairs leading to the basement below. He switched on the flashlight, found the keyhole, and tried the first of four keys on Caspar's ring. The door clicked open on the second try, and Nicholas stepped carefully down the steeply pitched stairs, guided by the rays of his light. The hodgepodge of furniture brought a tiny groan to his lips, but he moved stealthily toward the corner he thought lay directly below Caspar's desk on the floor above. Old crates, lengths of wood, and parts of tables and chairs had been stacked there haphazardly, forming a nearly impenetrable thicket. It might take hours to search through it all. Desperate, he swung the light upward to the low ceiling, trying to remember the precise location of the desk.

He saw it then, just barely—a fine wire that ran down from the ceiling and was lost in the darkness below. Of course! He tipped the beam and followed the line of the wire down to a small cardboard box. Propping the light on an adjacent crate, he carefully lifted the flaps of the container and bent forward to inspect the tiniest tape recorder he had ever seen.

He never heard Planchet, who rose from the crate behind him, hammer in hand.

Caspar snored gently.

"Out like a light," breathed Wren. "If I had to kiss him one more time, I'd have handed in my goddamn resignation. He doesn't shave, and he doesn't wash a lot, either. He smells a little like spoiled garlic."

"You did very nicely, my dear," said Tewksbury, locking the door.

"A life of crime is no picnic, I'll say that. What now?"

"We'll join Nicholas downstairs. I want to return this key to the ring, and Nicholas may need a bit of help. Let's go see."

They tiptoed carefully down the stairs and back along the hall to the basement stairs. Peering down, Wren could see the faintest of glows.

"I see his light," she whispered. "Look, professor, it's

damn dark down there, and these stairs are steep. You lay chickie here and I'll go down and see if Nick wants any help."

"Lay chickie?"

"Make like a sentry!" she hissed, and started down.

The old man stifled his objections. "Very well. But do hurry, my dear."

Wren worked her way cautiously toward the faint glow in the rear corner. There it was—the flashlight, propped on a crate. She smiled with relief, took a confident step forward, squarely onto the back of Nick's outflung hand. She stumbled awkwardly for a moment, and as Nicholas groaned, Wren screamed sharply and fell softly across his body in a dead faint.

"The young man is not dead, then? You're quite certain, Peel?"

"No doubt about it, Mr. Swain. Planchet knows his business, sir."

"The equipment . . . ?"

"All out, Mr. Swain."

"Well done, Peel. I think it's time you took a short trip to Holland and . . . Belgium, Peel. A buying trip for tulip bulbs, shall we say? You'll want to spend a day or two in Bruges. At the usual place. Wait there for me, Peel. But make no contact with Tewksbury or his friends. Understood?"

Roland Swain replaced the phone, lifting the instrument and placing it carefully into the right-hand drawer of his desk. He locked it, as always, and pressed the button to summon the butler.

"Yes, sir?"

"A brief holiday, Hodd. Pack a small bag for me, there's a good chap. The gray tweed, I think. Two or three shirts; the usual drill. I'll leave directly you've packed."

*   *   *

Nicholas moaned and opened his eyes. The morning sun filled the hotel room. Painfully he turned his head, to find Wren studying him.

"My head . . . my . . . *hand.* Wha-what happened?"

"You were bopped," said Wren.

"I think I'm dying," said Nicholas. He felt at the back of his head and winced. "My god. I've got a lump as big as a walnut back there."

"Walnuts aren't so damn big," said Wren grimly. "Tennis balls are a lot bigger."

"Warm and sympathetic," mumbled Nicholas, "that's what I like about you."

"She's been mother-henning you most of the night, Nicholas," said the professor. He had been standing at the window, looking down at the quiet street below. He turned to join Wren by the side of the bed. "Miss Wooding has worried about you, and so have I. Adventuring is one thing, but I must say I hadn't counted on violence. And you were tapped by a very professional hand, my boy. I've worried about that, too. Such a pity you never had a chance to see him. Whoever it was, I mean."

"Whoever-it-was also cleaned out the microphone and the tape recorder," said Wren. "Someone else wanted it out of there more than we did."

"Will I have a scar?" said Nicholas.

"The flesh is barely broken, my boy. You are a tough nut to crack, I must say. What about your hand? Can you move it?"

Nicholas wiggled his fingers cautiously. "It hurts, but if I can move it, nothing's broken." He frowned. "What did he hit me on the hand for?"

"I stepped on it," said Wren.

"Well. That's different." He looked at them with a crooked grin. "Well, gang, we wanted the bugs out, and they're out. Caspar remains our carefree cabinetmaker. He starts today. Let's pay a call on him."

"I'm not so sure," said Wren doubtfully. "Even money we're being bugged or watched. Maybe we ought to stay away from Caspar for a while."

"Not a chance," said Nicholas. "For one thing, we have to bring Caspar the first half of his money, or nothing happens, remember? And if we're bugged, they'll hear all this anyway. *Tempus* has a way of *fugit*-ing. I'll get dressed."

"I agree with Nicholas, my dear," said Tewksbury. "He is our leader, you know. And the feeling grows on me that our friends, whoever they may be, are willing for us to proceed with Caspar. For the moment, at least."

"You two make me laugh," said Wren. "Ho-ho-ho. You keep talking about Whoever-it-was and Our Friends and sneak your little looks at *me*. It's our old devil Roland Swain you're worried about, isn't it? What are you trying to do? Keep me from worrying? Me? The big gem buyer from Boston?" Her face twisted, and tears rolled down her cheeks. "I'm not worried, goddamnit!"

"Then what are you crying about?" said Nicholas.

"Because I'm *worried*," she sobbed.

Twelve

"Good morning," said Caspar. "Pretty morning, no?" He made a little show of gallantry, helping Wren over a nonexistent step, then walked nimbly through the shop toward his office. "I feel ve-ry good, Lewis Tewksbury. Your wine, yes? Ho, but I had so *much* to drink!" He paused and turned to regard Wren shyly. "I think I give you the kiss. Always, with wine, the red hair of a beautiful woman excites. Did I offend?"

"*Au contraire,*" said Wren bravely. "You were most charming."

"*Charmant,*" he instructed her.

"Right. *Charmant.*"

"You are so kind. Come, sit down, and we shall talk."

Nicholas moved to the chair at the corner of the desk and felt surreptitiously for the microphone. It was no longer there, just as he'd been told. "It feels so smooth," he murmured. "I have the first payment right here, Mr. Van der Ek, as we agreed."

The cabinetmaker picked up the brown envelope, thick with currency, and riffled the bills once.

"Thank you," he said to Nicholas. "But you do not look so good this morning, I think. The wine last night?"

Nicholas fingered his lump. "I don't have the head for it, I guess."

Professor Tewksbury cleared his throat hastily. "May we proceed to our business? If you will allow me, there are some preliminary thoughts I wish to share with you."

"A lecture," said Wren. "Just like at school. Beautiful."

"Some questions, my dear, for Caspar. If you don't mind?"

Caspar nodded affably. "But yes. There is much you can tell me and—perhaps—a few things I have myself learned."

"You are too modest," said Tewksbury. "To be brief, I think that we all want to be very sure that we avoid every possible risk of detection and exposure. Our designs are authentic, yes. Our ebony and ivory and the rest, also authentic. So we start with the wood for our *bureau du roi.* The carcass."

"Oak," said Caspar. "*Pedunculata,* perfectly seasoned."

"And the veneer?"

"Mahogany."

"Old Spanish timber, imported from Honduras, do you think?"

Caspar shrugged. "Probably. It has the grain."

"I thought mahogany was mahogany," said Wren.

"Hardly," said the professor. "The mahoganies from Guatemala or Nicaragua or Africa are all quite distinctive. The Honduran wood was much the preferred."

"Our wood is perfect," said the cabinetmaker firmly. "You will see."

"And the tools?"

"My tools are much like those used by Jesus Christ when He was a carpenter. Well . . . except for the marquetry saw, perhaps. Chisel, file, adze, ruler, scraper, router—they have changed very little in two thousand years."

"Fantastic," said Wren.

"No power tools, mind. They leave signs that could sink us all."

"Agreed, of course."

"Your marquetry saw—a hand tool also?"

"Listen," said Wren, "what are you planning? Inlay or marquetry? It's kind of crucial."

Unexpectedly, Caspar nodded. "Yes. I too have the question about the marquetry, professor." Tewkbury's eyes widened in surprise. "I explain," said Caspar. "We call it marquetry because the inlay covers the whole surface of the table or the whole front of the cabinet—complete. So. From Paris, you bring me these beautiful paper designs by Oeben and Riesener. I use the very small needles, yes? I make the small holes in the paper, following every line on it. Then, with the small rag ball I push the fine powder—the bitumen powder—through each hole onto the ebony. It makes the powder lines. I bake them to the surface with the hot plate . . . and *voilà!* I am ready to cut. You follow?"

Wren nodded.

"Good. Already, I have sliced the ebony, the ivory, the pearl, the tortoise—like the slices of the bread, eh? Like so." He held up a thumb and forefinger, an eighth of an inch apart. "Thin, like this. I take the four slices, glue them together, like the sandwich—with my powdered lines on top, so I can see them! I cut the pretty jasmine flower, perhaps, or the leaf, the stem, the vase, the ribbon, the butterfly, the bird. With each cut, I make four—ebony, ivory, shell, and pearl. Little by little, I cover the whole surface. You understand?"

111

"Sure," said Wren. "So what puzzles you? You sound as if you know what you're doing."

"Ah! The designs you bring from Paris are not the true marquetry! The whole surface is not covered. Only part! You see? Do we make the great error, Lewis Tewksbury?"

The professor applauded softly. "Very good, Caspar. Very good indeed. Our buyer will raise the question, of course. He will summon his expert. The expert will summon another expert. Let me tell you what they will say. Design? Oeben and Riesener, clearly. Wood? Authentic. Marquetry? Aha! Oeben was very partial to elaborate marquetry; most of his works were covered with it. But not all of them, Caspar, not all. Very early on, Riesener began to produce surfaces with cleaner, simpler designs. He chose to display the superb grains of the veneers, not to cover them. The experts know this. They will see our desk here and think of other desks—also with more restrained use of inlay—and also signed by both Oeben and Riesener. They will talk. Was this work produced by Riesener when Oeben was alive? The queen, Marie Antoinette, preferred the simpler designs, you know. Or was it produced by Riesener after Oeben died, but signed by *both* names, as Riesener was known to do?" Tewksbury grinned. "They cannot know. It is precisely this ambiguity that makes this little writing desk the perfect choice. The experts will make their tests. No modern tools. Old veneer. Superb workmanship. All this they will report to the collector, accept their fee, and depart."

"They will not suspect the surface?" said Caspar.

"On the contrary, my friend. It will support our case very nicely."

"I also have the rare woods, many of them, Lewis Tewksbury. They were used for decoration, for borders. I am to use them? Rosewood I have. Also satinwood, laburnum, dark walnut, olive, cherry, many more."

"With discretion, with restraint, yes. If one is not so old,

you may do as Oeben did. Stain it gently, or scorch it, perhaps."

"Scorch what?" asked Wren. "How?"

"With the small iron, red hot," said Caspar. "This I know
well. The wood I toast to the soft brown. It is . . . what is
the word, please, professor?"

"Charring, Caspar. You char the wood—also gently."

"Just so. It makes the *ombre,* the shadow effect." He
reached for the brown envelope. "Well, then. I must begin.
There is much to do."

"How long is all this going to take?" said Wren. "A year or
something?"

The cabinetmaker stared at her. "A year? No, no, not so
much as the year. Riesener made twelve like this in the
year. Our *bureau du roi* will be complete in four weeks.
Less, if all goes well."

"If. There's that word again," said Nicholas.

From just inside the door to the great cathedral, Roland
Swain watched Wren, Nicholas, and the old professor walk
slowly across the open square toward their hotel.

"That's the lot," said Peel.

"The man and the woman are younger than I'd expected. But, yes, that is the famous Lewis Tewksbury, beyond
doubt." He glanced at his watch. "They shall be lunching
very soon. You have your man ready to move?"

"As to that, Mr. Swain, here I am, and they are here—
and I thought I'd take care of this myself. Make sure of it,
so to speak."

Swain nodded. "Just as you say. No slips, mind you."

"Me, sir?" Peel looked modestly down to his hands, and
flexed them gracefully. "Not bloody likely."

"Trout for lunch was a definite mistake," said Wren faintly. "I'm in no mood to look at cooked eyes."

"It isn't just the queen's letter we'll want them to discover in the secret drawer," said Nicholas. "A workshop record, maybe."

"It was the wine last night. Then, too, I was up all night watching your walnut." Wren sighed.

"No, not a workshop record. Too pat, my boy," said Tewksbury. "It will have to be the sort of document the queen would want to keep hidden away."

"What I really need is a nap," said Wren. "Will you excuse me, gentlemen?"

"Then there's the matter of paper and ink," said Nicholas.

Wren tapped the side of the drinking glass with her spoon. They looked up. "I'm going up to the room to take a nap, fellow criminals. My head aches. It's hard to be a wino. But you carry on. If the vote splits one to one, I vote yes, whatever the hell it is."

She took the miniature elevator to the third floor. Reaching her room, she rooted for the key in her shoulder pouch.

Peel touched her lightly on the shoulder as she entered. The switchblade, all five inches of it, sprang from its slot. He laid the flat side of it against Wren's throat.

"We'll go down by the service lift, miss," he said softly, "and out the rear door. You be nice and quiet and you'll not be hurt."

"Wow," said Wren. "Can I get some aspirin first?"

Thirteen

"What you must try to understand," said Roland Swain, "is that my Mr. Peel is a sort of thinking weapon. I never carry arms myself. They provoke violence, and I dislike violence. Mr. Peel is my weapon, and for the moment, your young lady is quite safe, I assure you."

Tewksbury's face was pink with outrage. "If you harm one hair on her head, I'll . . . I'll—"

"I have no such intention," said Swain, cutting in. "And I need only remind you that if *I* am harmed, Mr. Peel has his instructions. Come, now. Let us exchange no more of these unpleasant threats. Shall I pour?"

Wren had disappeared not three hours ago. Discovering her absence, Nicholas had first scoured the hotel, and then, in growing alarm, had raced to Tewksbury's room. Swain's message, delivered by the bellhop, arrived while they were trying to make sense of it all.

Shall we meet in the lobby for tea at five? It was signed with the single letter *S*.

Roland Swain paid much attention to his tea, tipping a bit of milk into the brew, then adding a touch of sugar. He tasted it judiciously.

"Fortnum's, I think," he said, "and just the way I like it."

"What do you want?" said Nicholas. Masking the turmoil that caused his heart to pound, he sipped his tea, voice calm, hand steady.

Swain dabbed at his lips with the napkin. "Two things, actually. First, to inform you of the realities of this matter that brings you to Bruges. Second, to extend a certain suggestion. We can chat here quite safely, I think. No microphones, this time." His eyes toured the hotel's lounge. "Nice and private," he murmured.

"What realities?" said Nicholas.

"To say it plainly, young man, you and your friends have invaded my territory. Others have tried it, of course. I say to you now what I have said to them. My associates and I control the fake-antique market. We function somewhat beyond the limits of the law, so the conventional recourse to the police and to the courts is not available to us. In consequence, we have learned to administer our own law—and the punishment for its transgression."

"That's a lot of words."

"True," said Swain, "but hardly idle ones. Your young lady might be found in one of the canals here, quite dead. Mr. Peel has my orders to smother her quickly and drop her in. He will do so. You must understand that. He has done so for me many, many times. Not just idle words, you see."

"It sounds excessive," said Nicholas. "We can hardly be classified as significant competition."

"No competition is insignificant." Swain's tone was bleak. "We may be . . . excessive, as you say. But we must, you see. There are more than two hundred little fish that we manage. If we allowed one of them—Caspar, in this case—to go swimming off on his own, it might encourage others to follow him. Men are greedy, and our net must be mended and watched constantly. No, the reality is this: we can permit no competition that uses our people."

"Kidnapping, intimidation, threats of murder! You are a parasite," gritted Tewksbury, "creating nothing, fattening on the talent of others, selling fraudulent goods. An outrage!"

"I don't agree at all, sir," said Nicholas thoughtfully. "Mr. Swain does what we do, really. He makes and sells copies for money. He does it as a professional, and he does it successfully. He's taken Wren, sure. But only to immobilize us. It seems to me that he's better at this than we are. It's a matter of common sense."

Roland Swain stared at Nicholas.

"A matter of . . . common sense. Well, well. What is your name, young man?"

"Nicholas. Nicholas Otter."

"Otter. Lovely animals. I might say, Mr. Otter, that you put my case better than I do myself."

Tewksbury rose, pale with fury. "I'll have no more to do with this." Turning on Nicholas, his voice bitter, he said, "You disappoint me, Nicholas. I had not thought to find you a Judas."

"Sit down, professor," said Nicholas curtly. "We're in this together. We'll listen to Mr. Swain together. You're an old man, professor. For god's sake, try not to be old-fashioned. Just sit and listen."

"You are *full* of surprises, Mr. Otter. I had assumed that Professor Tewksbury led your little band. I see that I was mistaken. You, then, are in command?"

"He is, damnit," said Tewksbury. "The whole idea was his."

"And the young lady, Miss . . . ?"

"Wooding," said Nicholas. "Wren Wooding. She had the seed money, Mr. Swain."

"Not bad," murmured Swain. "Tewksbury for the scholarship. Miss Wooding for the finance. And my friend Caspar to do the work. In fact, young man, very good indeed. I compliment you."

"But not good enough," said Nicholas. "How did you get on to us—if you don't mind my asking, I mean."

"Let us say that I make it a policy to have my people watched. As a matter of interest, Mr. Otter, I often have my *watchers* watched."

"That would be Mr. Busset?"

"You know about Busset, of course. The professor had quite a nice talk with him. I had the report in a matter of hours."

Nicholas shook his head slowly, his admiration plain. "That's the difference. *Organization.*" He sighed. "We never really had a chance, did we?"

Silence settled around them. Roland Swain studied Nicholas, unblinking. The professor shifted uneasily in his chair.

"What I like about your *bureau du roi* is the scope of it, Mr. Otter," said Swain at last. "It appeals to me. We've done very well with smaller—and less demanding—reproductions. We are organized for volume. I've avoided these major projects because the risks are so high. And the expense."

"For seven hundred thousand dollars, I thought the risk worth taking," said Nicholas.

"The U.S. market rarely goes quite that high, however." Swain pulled softly at his lower lip. "Rarely, I'd say."

"I saw one like ours that sold for just under seven hundred thousand dollars—just a few weeks ago. In New York, at Gilliat's."

"You know the American market, it seems."

Nicholas nodded.

"I think I'm going to make my suggestion now, Mr. Otter. Nothing firm, mind you. But let's see where it might lead us. Instead of stopping your plan and sending you home, I'm wondering if you might like to continue on?"

"Are you proposing a partnership?" said Tewksbury. "If so, our answer is an unequivocal *no*! I say—"

Nicholas broke in quickly. "You hold Wren, so you hold the cards, Mr. Swain. We've invested the best part of her inheritance in this thing, and I'd like to get it back. Yes. I'd like to continue on . . . and so would the professor, when he starts thinking again."

"No partnership, I'm afraid," said Swain. "But you'll find my terms generous. I pride myself on that."

"Go on."

"Your writing table—how did you propose to sell it?"

"Gilliat's."

Swain nodded. "I agree completely. Therefore, ten percent to them, and ten percent to you on the remaining balance, plus anything over seven hundred thousand dollars."

"And a half-million dollars to you—for doing nothing," snapped the professor.

"Slow down," said Nicholas. "Think about what Mr. Swain is saying. It's a chance to get Wren's money back. It's also a chance to walk away with some profit. The way things stand right now, we walk away empty-handed." He turned to Swain. "I like the sound of it. You've also started me off on a new line of thinking. I'd like a little time to chew on it, if I may. And I'd like to talk to Wren about it, too. So I guess I have to ask you if you're willing to release her?"

Swain waved his hand negligently. "But of course, Mr. Otter. You'll find me a very reasonable man . . . and I give you my word that Miss Wooding is quite safe. I hold

my Mr. Peel on a very tight leash." He studied his watch.
I'll have her back here in the hotel, safe and sound, in less
than an hour. You see? Nothing to worry about."

"It's not me that's worried, Mr. Swain. But Wren—Miss
Wooding—worries a lot. . . ."

"What are you going to do to me?" said Wren. "If it's torture, I'll talk, believe me. I've got this splitting headache.
Torture on top of this headache would be just too much,
you know?"

Peel looked properly shocked. "*Torture* you, miss? I do
not torture young women; not Alexander Peel."

"What *do* you do, then? Specialize in girl-napping?"

"Girl-napping? Ah, yes. I see. Very funny, that. No,
miss, I'm by way of being your skilled professional killer, as
they say."

"Really? You're not joking?" Wren studied him carefully.
"I don't believe it. You look like the owner of a gift shop or
something."

"Flower shop, it is. Very close, that. You're smart as new
paint, if I may say so."

"*C'mon,*" said Wren. "People who own flower shops
don't go around killing people. You're trying to frighten
me, so I'll talk. Right?"

Peel dug a finger into his ear and scratched. His mild eyes
surveyed Wren.

"Je-zuzz. You really mean it, don't you?"

Peel nodded.

"Wow. You've got a way about you, Mr. Peel, I'll say
that. Ask your questions. No goddamn desk is worth trad-
ing for a coffin."

"Ah, but we know about your writing table already,
miss."

"The little microphone. Yours?"

"Smart, like I say."

"I'm a hostage, then?"

"That you are."

"I think I get it. I'm Roland Swain's insurance policy, right? You hold me while he meets Nicholas and the professor and puts the screws on."

"Ve-ry good, miss. Yes, if Mr. Swain comes to any harm, so do you, I'm afraid."

Wren laughed. "I'm as safe as I can be, Mr. Peel. By god, you make me feel a hell of a lot better. I know my Nicholas!" She surveyed the room more carefully. Stone walls, whitewashed so often that the corners were rounded. One small window, barred. A stout door. Narrow bed, blue blanket, small pillow, two straight-backed chairs.

"Where are we, anyway, Mr. Peel—if I'm allowed to know."

Peel smiled. "About twenty minutes from Bruges, miss, on the road to Zeebrugge."

"Listen," said Wren, "this may sound weird, but I never met a real professional killer. It fascinates me, it really does. Could we talk about it? I may never get another chance."

"Afraid not, miss. My work is very confidential-like."

"Not about any others, Mr. Peel. *Me!* How would . . . I mean, would you use that awful knife?"

"My knife? Not at all, miss. Too messy, knives are. No, my little knife convinces people to do just as I tell them, and to do it quickly and with no noise. As for you, miss, just a pillow over your face. Very little pain, that way. No noise, no blood. Very neat, as you say, miss. I like to work neatly, if I do say so myself."

Wren rose and walked to the bed, lifting the pillow. "This one? This would do it?"

Peel nodded affably. "Indeed it would. Just about the right size."

"But, I mean, wouldn't there be a struggle? What do you do? Drug my coffee? Knock me out with a bang on the head? Or would you do it while I was sleeping?"

"You're a cool one," said Peel. "You've no idea how

some of my clients carry on. The tears? Floods! Begging
and bribes—you've just no idea."

"Yes, Mr. Peel, but *how?*"

"In the corner, there, miss. I like to work in a corner. Not
so much mucking about in a corner, if you see what I
mean."

Wren carried the pillow over to one of the corners of the
room and backed into the angle. "Right. Show me, Mr.
Peel. I mean, not for real. Just for demonstration. I've never seen a real professional. Will you? *Please?*" She held out
the pillow.

Peel shrugged and rose to his feet. "I'll do it, but you be
careful, mind? We don't want to hold it too close, or for too
long. You *are* sure you want me to show you?"

"Hell yes," said Wren, grinning. "Why not? How many
people really know what a true artist does when he works in
your business?"

Peel nodded and took the pillow. Spreading his legs just a
bit, he leaned his chest against Wren's body, pinning her
arms with his own and placing the pillow lightly—but
firmly—over her face.

It was then that Wren brought her knee up sharply into
his groin, driving it, just as she'd been taught, straight into
his testicles and doubling him over in agony. Locking her
two hands, she held them high over the nape of the exposed neck and brought them down in a powerful, prac-
ticed motion.

Peel blacked out. His knees unlocked, and he fell softly,
his face partially resting on the pillow.

Je-zuzz, thought Wren. *It actually works.*

Nicholas and the professor watched Roland Swain take
his neat little steps down the stairs to the sidewalk. A parked
car rolled slowly forward, its door swinging open. Swain
climbed in.

Tewksbury let the curtain fall back into place. "I'm not a betting man, my boy, but I'd wager that was our Mr. Planchet at the wheel."

"Did you get it all?" asked Nicholas.

"I hope so, my boy. It's a small recorder, I grant you. But taped to the inner side of my thigh, it makes one hell of an uncomfortable lump. I worried constantly that I'd cross my legs and push one of the wrong buttons."

"You were fine, professor. It was the smallest I could get on short notice. You take that reel and stick it somewhere under one of your shirts or something. I've got a refill in my room; I'll get it." He struck a palm with his tightly clenched fist. "I'm going to *nail* that son of a bitch, professor. That's a promise!"

"There's very little on this recording you could take into a court of law, Nicholas. Without incriminating all of us, that is. You see that, don't you?"

"Court of law?" said Nicholas slowly. "Who said anything about a court of law? Roland Swain took Wren and threatened to have her smothered to *death*. That's all I need to know."

"If you kill him, Nicholas, you're no better than he is."

"I know that, professor. I'm not going to kill him. I've got a better idea than that. I really do."

Tewksbury sighed. "I'm happier to hear that than I can tell you. I'm off, then. You bring the new tape right on up. Wren should be along very soon now. We'll play it for her, too. She'll like that part where you call me old-fashioned, damn you." The old man smiled and moved toward the elevator.

"You're on the fifth floor. I'm on three. I'll take the stairs," said Nicholas.

Minutes later, he unlocked the door and stood there, his jaw slack.

"Hi," said Wren. She was in bed, the lamp on, reading.

"How the hell did *you* get back so fast? Swain left here no more than five minutes ago! What did he do, phone ahead? Or . . . wait a minute! *Have you been in the hotel all the time?*"

"I keep saying you think too much. Also, you can't use the bathtub."

"What's that supposed to mean?"

"You can't use the goddamn bathtub," said Wren patiently, "because it's being used."

"Listen, Wren, I've had a hell of a day. I've been worried half out of my mind because of you. My walnut is killing me. We had a fantastic meeting with Swain. Now, where have you *been*? And what's all this crud about the bathtub?"

"Have a look, Admiral. I've brought you a little surprise."

Shaking his head, Nicholas strode to the door of the bathroom and flung it open. *There was a man in the bathtub.* Fully dressed, bound hand and foot, with his mouth stuffed with one of Wren's panties; a redheaded man who glared at him with rage, struggling fruitlessly to lift himself to a sitting position.

"Who the fuck is that?" hissed Nicholas over his shoulder.

"Mr. Peel," said Wren. "He's the one who captured me."

"How did he get *here*, for Christ's sake?"

"I brought him. You don't think he wanted to come, do you?"

"Yeah, yeah, but how did you do it?"

"Kung fu," said Wren. "My course in self-defense. Remember?" She got out of bed and came over to the doorway. "I kicked him in the balls, actually."

"That's not kung fu. Come on."

"Right in the balls. Al Pacino did it to Robert De Niro once, in a picture. Or maybe it was the other way around—or somebody else. Anyway, he's our hostage."

Peel's face turned a bright scarlet as he struggled. Low grunts, muffled by the panties, erupted from his throat.

"Why can't he sit up?"

"I've got about six feet of adhesive tape around the faucet, connected to his wrists."

"Let me get this straight. You brought him back to the hotel, right?"

"Bang on. In his own car. It's in the alley, behind the hotel."

"You carried him?"

"Well, I dragged him. And he's a bitch to tote around, too."

"Anybody see you?"

"What do you think I am—some amateur? Of course nobody saw me. He lurked and skulked when he took me out of here, so I lurked and skulked when I brought him back."

"And he's the one who was going to smother you? Alexander Peel?" Nicholas stared down into the bathtub, his face pale.

Peel's struggles stopped.

"A hostage," murmured Nicholas. He closed the door and headed for the telephone at the bedside. "I'm calling the professor. We need a meeting of the board of directors."

"I'll tell you one thing," said Wren. "My headache is all gone."

Fourteen

They carried Peel into the bedroom and sat him down on one of the armchairs. "We've had a meeting about you," said Nicholas, "and here's what we're going to do. First, I'm going to take this thing out of your mouth." Nicholas paused as Peel nodded energetically. "That's if you agree not to make a fuss. You start to shout or something, and back in it goes. You follow?"

Peel nodded again, his eyes imploring.

"Right," said Nicholas. "Now, there's a lot of adhesive tape that holds it in, so it's going to hurt. You ready?" The sticky tape came away reluctantly, tugging at the flesh of Peel's cheeks and plucking strands of his hair as Nicholas peeled it off. Their prisoner hacked once, and the panties popped out of his mouth. This was followed by a spasm of gasps and coughing.

"Water!" croaked Peel.

Wren lifted the decanter and was about to pour, when Nicholas restrained her gently. "Not yet. He has to do some talking first."

"The man can hardly talk unless you give him a bit of water," said Tewksbury reasonably.

Nicholas shook his head, looking straight at Peel. "He thinks we're soft. He has to understand that you may be soft, and Wren may be soft. But not me." He slipped Peel's switchblade knife from his pocket. "Or are you forgetting what I found in his pocket, professor?" The menacing blade leaped out with a click, and Peel's head pulled back, his eyes fixed on the knife.

"You talk—you get to drink. It's that simple, Peel. I'm not going to cut you up." Nicholas bent down, his nose bare inches from the bound man. He spoke very slowly. "What I'm *going* to do is to take you out into the country tonight and hide you, Mr. Peel. I'll gag you and tie you with every inch of adhesive tape we've got left . . . and you'll never be found. *I'm going to let you starve to death, you son of a bitch.* As God is my witness, that's a promise."

"You frighten me," said Wren, "but I'm not sure you frighten him."

Peel's lips, parched and dry, worked. "I . . . I believe him, miss. Before God, I do."

"If I let you drink, you'll talk? You'll answer some questions?"

Peel's eyes studied Nicholas. "I don't have a ruddy choice, do I? I'll talk."

Wren filled a glass and held it to his lips, tilting it slowly. She poured another, and he drank again, greedily.

"I still say it's a mistake," grumbled Nicholas. "But go ahead, professor. He's all yours."

Professor Tewksbury pulled an empty chair around, so that it faced Peel squarely.

"Nicholas is furious with you," he said, sitting. "The fact

is that he voted to . . . dispose of you. Miss Wooding and I have been able to persuade him to be patient. We think we can work out a treaty of peace with Mr. Swain. We're prepared to be reasonable, if he's prepared to be reasonable. You follow?"

"My balls are killing me," said Peel.

"No doubt," said Tewksbury, "but you haven't answered my question."

"I may be permanently damaged. Sterilized, like they say."

"I assure you that a knee in the scrotum, though painful indeed, will not sterilize you, Mr. Peel."

Peel's face mirrored a vast relief. "You wouldn't lie about a thing like that, now, would you, professor?"

"My word on it, as a gentleman."

"By god, but she has a kick like a horse, and that's the truth."

"The point is, Mr. Peel, that we want you to help us to set up a peace conference with Mr. Swain. Are you prepared to assist us?"

Peel shifted uneasily. "You won't like to hear this, professor, but I'm not much use to you as a hostage. Mr. Swain doesn't give a damn for me. Not really. What I mean is, he'll *say* he's sorry to lose me. But he's a hard man, Mr. Swain is, and if holding me is supposed to persuade him . . . well, I'm for it."

"Oh, good!" said Wren.

"It doesn't mean that, my dear," said the professor. "It's rather—as we might say—'We've had it.'"

"Too right," said Peel.

"We're inclined to agree," said Tewksbury. "The kind of man who would order you to smother a helpless young woman must be, by definition, ruthless."

"Helpless?" said Peel. "Her?"

"Nevertheless," said Tewksbury, "we think it wise to add a bit of weight to our side of the scales, Mr. Peel."

"Meaning . . . what, sir?"

"Planchet, Mr. Peel. And Busset. We want them. We intend to isolate Mr. Swain. Capture his troops, as it were. What we want you to do is to call them on the telephone over here and instruct them to come to the hotel. Planchet first, then Busset. We've plenty of adhesive tape . . . and Miss Wooding will hold the phone for you."

"While I hold the knife," said Nicholas. "One wrong word, and I cut the cord, slap the gag back in, and take you away. You ready?"

"Well, not quite," said Peel. He stole a quick glance at Wren. "Excuse me for saying so, miss, but I have to go to the bathroom." His voice went soft with intense embarrassment. "Number one," he muttered.

"The phone I will hold for him," said Wren, "but that is *it*."

"You've taken all this very well," said the professor. "Indeed, you surprise me. No anger, no argument? No threats? Amazing."

Roland Swain shrugged. "What am I to do?" he said. "You have somehow managed to take the only three men available to me in Bruges. You've trussed them up like geese, though how you managed Mr. Peel I cannot begin to imagine. Mr. Otter here plucked me out of my little house with that terrible knife he carries . . ." Swain turned to Nicholas. "I've tried to convince you that my intentions have been peaceable, Mr. Otter. When I invited you and your colleagues to continue on your project with Caspar, I meant it very sincerely. Truly I did."

"Too much sincerity," said Nicholas harshly. "Peel had your orders to kill Wren. You told us so yourself."

Swain shook his head impatiently. "You disappoint me. The threat was made, yes. But only to safeguard my own person. Ask yourself honestly. Would you have jeopardized the young lady's life? Would you have allowed her to die? I say you would *not*. I counted on it, Mr. Otter, and I'll tell you why. You wanted her alive . . . and so did I. I found the prospect of half a million dollars very impressive. Kill Miss Wooding? I'd be the worst kind of fool to do so!"

"That's your stock in trade," said Nicholas. "Making a fake sound like the real thing. You look sincere, you sound sincere. Who the hell knows, you may even *be* sincere—right now. But I'll ask you a question. How long would I last if you were in my shoes? I'll tell you. About as long as it would take for you to unhook Peel's leash. And you know it!"

"I'm going to teach you something, young man. About negotiations. When a game like this begins, there are never more than three things to think about. Is one destined to win? Or to lose?" Swain paused and held up a finger. "Or to *compromise?*" he said softly. "If you had chosen to kill me, you could have done so easily. I'm an old man. I'm unarmed. You hold my men. But here I am—alive. And despite Peel and Planchet, there *you* are—alive. You are not destined to win, therefore, nor am I. What remains?"

Tewksbury nodded. "I agree, Nicholas. I do not care very much for Mr. Swain, but the force of what he says cannot be denied. We have his men down in your room. We have him here, in mine. And I will remind you that Miss Wooding and I favor some sort of compromise. Then, too, I think Mr. Becker's opinion must be taken into account."

"Becker is in Boston," said Nicholas, "and I'm getting goddamn tired of clearing every move we make with Mr. Peerless Leader Becker!" He spoke with an intensity that caused Swain's eyes to narrow thoughtfully.

"Calm down," said Wren. "This is a Becker Operation

because Becker is an operator. Would we be here if he hadn't given me the money? Would we be here if Becker hadn't told us how to set this up?" She leaned forward, lowering her voice. "After all, we can always call in . . ." Wren looked at Swain. "We can always call in the little fat Turkish guy with the big yacht, right?"

"You talk too much," said Nicholas.

"Becker?" said Swain. "I know of no such name. And who is this Turk? Are you trying to suggest that there exists some other organization about which I know nothing? What nonsense is this?"

Nicholas stared at Roland Swain coldly.

"You said it yourself, Mr. Swain. You're an old man. You know the U.S. market, but do you operate there? You do not. Any agents? Any distributors? Any *anything*? You're nickels and dimes, Mr. Swain. You have this funny little network you're so proud of—probably in a card file in your bottom desk drawer, next to your secret telephone. You have a ding-a-ling crew of old parties like Caspar Van der Ek in six or seven countries, and you make some money on your tourist-junk fakes. Becker is solid gold, Mr. Swain. Computerized, with market segmentations, seasonal variations, demographic mixes—the works."

"Trend lines," said Wren. "Don't forget them."

"Right," said Nicholas. "I'll tell you what infuriates me about you, Mr. Swain. You're blind with your smugness. You remind me of the stylops—a tiny parasitic insect who lives inside the body of the honeybee—and someone comes along and says, 'Hey! There's a big world out there!' And all you can say is, 'Some other world about which I know nothing? What nonsense is this?'"

Swain pulled thoughtfully at his lip.

"If you're wondering if it's possible that you *might* be mistaken, the answer is yes," said Nicholas. "Becker is big money, Mr. Swain. Big enough to keep Professor Tewksbury on his payroll, if you're interested. We work for Becker, all of us. *I* work for him—at least, up until now."

"Now who's talking too much?" said Wren.

"I don't give a good goddamn," said Nicholas. "Becker is like Swain here, only bigger. All take, no give. I'm pulling out."

"What about the project?" asked Wren.

"The table? I've done the work, so I'm taking *it*, too. If Mr. Becker decides to get nasty, I'll call . . . I'll call my friend in Turkey."

"I'm tempted to join you, Nicholas," said Tewksbury. "But I do not like violence. You know that."

"Then stay out," said Nicholas.

"Will you do this, Nicholas? Will you call Mr. Becker? Will you tell him plainly that you and I—and Miss Wooding too, I'm almost certain—have decided to go into business for ourselves, that we resign from the Becker organization, but that we will return his initial investment and a fair share of the proceeds? If he rejects this eminently fair offer, then you may alert our Turkish colleague."

"I agree," said Wren. "You call Becker and tell him that the three of us hang together, so that we make damn sure we do not hang separately."

"What—ah—what about the four of us," said Roland Swain.

Wren lowered her eyes, to mask the tingle of excitement that coursed through her body. *Goddamn,* she thought, *we actually hooked the old bastard!*

Nicholas shook his head firmly. "What do we need Swain for?"

Swain made as though to speak, only to be interrupted by Tewksbury. "It's very late," the old professor said. "I'm quite tired. Let us take one careful step forward. Let us agree to meet tomorrow morning for breakfast and a little more talk. Shall we? You will spend the night here in the hotel, Mr. Swain?"

"No objections, of course," said Swain.

"You've got twin beds," said Nicholas, "so he can sleep here. Hand me the adhesive, Wren. We tie him down, god-damnit. Until he's in—*if* he's in—he's out."

"Yes," said Roland Swain, "I can see that. It's the commonsense thing to do, really."

Wren and Nicholas walked slowly down the corridor of the hotel toward their room.

"How the hell are we going to get any sleep tonight?" said Wren. "Swain is tucked in with the professor, but we've got the three musketeers right in our room, and *I* don't want to be taking Peel to the bathroom all night."

Nicholas jingled the keys in his pocket and smiled. "The thing that makes a great pilot," he said, "is his ability to fly ahead of the plane, to think about where he's going to be before he gets there, see?"

"Sure. You're a great pilot. Why?"

"Because I went down to the lobby a while back and got us another room." He pulled a key from his pocket. "This here is what you call your basic extra room key."

Wren slipped her hand into his. "What a neat thing to do. What do I do then? Go to our old room first and pack a little bag?"

Nicholas shook his head. "We're only three doors down the hall. I've checked the boys and locked them in. So we move into our new digs."

"What about my toothbrush and my pajamas and my comb and all that?"

Nicholas slid the key into the lock. "To hell with all that. We sleep tonight with lots of skin rubbing around, and a couple of extra blankets."

"Wow," said Wren, "all of a sudden I feel erotic. It's wild. I feel as though you're taking me off to a hotel for a night of love, love, love."

"You just broke the code. Come on in."

"You know what Nicholas? I like it a lot when you're aggressive. Your trend line is definitely tilting up."

"That's a new word for it."

Fifteen

"It's a splendid plan," said the professor. "The more I think about it, the more convinced I am. Flawless and seamless, my boy."

"You were the key," said Nicholas. "Roland Swain bought the Becker idea because the famous Professor Lewis Tewksbury said he exists. Because Swain bought it, so did Peel and Planchet. It's that simple. Your fame, sir, turns out to be one hell of an asset."

"It's generous of you to say so. Nevertheless, the concept was yours and, in my judgment, is superb."

"We hope," said Nicholas. "A lot has to happen before we bank any money. A hell of a lot."

"I've got it," said Wren. "Pierre Planchet's face has been driving me nuts. He's a dead ringer for Alfred Hitchcock's brother, that's what he is! Double chin, pudding cheeks, puffy eyes—he's all Hitchcock." She reconsidered. "His younger brother."

"Yes," said the professor, "I see what you mean. But the important thing is that he believes Roland Swain . . . and Roland Swain told him that we are now partners. Planchet should make a very useful addition."

"As long as Peel watches him, and we watch Peel," agreed Nicholas.

"It was a good idea to let Busset pull out," said Wren. "He's a nervous criminal, and nervous criminals make me nervous. I think your successful criminal has to be basically calm." She smoothed her skirt and stood up. "I'm going to pay a call on Caspar. You two Harvard brains can sit in this hotel thinking major thoughts, but I need a little walk and some fresh air."

"Remarkable young woman," said Tewksbury, studying her retreating figure. "She reasons with impressive power. Cause-effect, problem-solution—that sort of thing. The more I see of her, the better I like her. Why don't you two get married?"

"I don't know," said Nicholas. "Too busy, I guess. Let's pin down this business with Planchet and Peel. They're off to London with Swain to line up our forged documents. If you're looking for flaws, think about that one, professor. I mean, can we trust them?"

"You recorded our meeting with them, didn't you?"
Nicholas nodded.

"Then we're prepared. In the ultimate, we can always scrap our project and take the tapes to the authorities. It all comes back to Swain, my boy. He's a wise old head, and as cautious as a turtle. You've teased him with a vista of riches, but it's my view that he'll start looking for our mysterious Carl Becker and our equally nonexistent Turkish friend just as soon as he reaches London. He'll come up empty-handed, of course. But will he conclude that Beck-

er's cover is so perfect that he can't be found, or will he begin to suspect that we've diddled him? I think greed will win
the day, my boy. In something over six or seven thousand
years of human history, it always has. No, I think you've
made a convert."

"I'm counting on the fact that he has damn few connec-
tions in the United States," said Nicholas.

"No, Nicholas. You count on greed. That's your lever-
age."

Nicholas shrugged. "We'll just have to wait and see. The
paper and the inks are supposed to be ready in a month."

"Perfect timing, too. I'm reasonably well qualified to
judge the paper and inks. Your letter from Marie Antoinette is simply perfect. If our luck holds, we'll have our
provenance at about the same time Caspar completes the
writing table."

"Again, if," said Nicholas. "Every time I hear that word,
my walnut throbs."

Caspar Van der Ek, beaming his pleasure, guided Wren
to his workbench. "I have started," he said happily. "The
veneer is even better than I knew. Look."

Wren whistled. "My god, it's breathtaking! It has a kind
of dark golden shine to it, doesn't it? That's the mahogany,
right?"

"Yes. From the mountains of Honduras. The trees were
cut by the Spanish two hundred years ago and brought to
Europe. See how delicate the grain is? How subtle? For two
hundred years the French finish has been darkening
slowly. Look, it is like soft gold. It is the finish of such wood
that Riesener wanted to show, and which Oeben covered
with his magnificent inlays."

"It seems like a crime to cut into it—for your secret compartments, I mean," said Wren. "Have you thought about
that?"

Caspar's eyes narrowed suspiciously.

"Wait a minute," Wren protested. "You don't have to tell me unless you want to. It's just that I had this idea. I thought you might like to know what it is, that's all."

"I make the promise to myself," said Caspar, somewhat mollified. "I wish to see if I can hide my little drawer so that not even the famous Lewis Tewksbury can find it—or open it. That is why I wish not to tell you what I think. Not yet, Mrs. Bird."

"Wren. Call me Wren. It's my first name. In fact . . . what the hell, Caspar. My real name is Wren Wooding. Okay?"

Caspar shook her hand solemnly. "It is good you have the trust. My name is also not Van der Ek—except for my other business. Allow me to introduce myself. My name is Caspar Planchet."

"Planchet? Same as Pierre Planchet?" She thought hard. "I remember! Your cousin, right?"

"My father's brother has the son, Pierre. And of course I will hear your idea, Mrs. Wooding."

"Miss," said Wren. "Nicholas and I are not married—at least not yet." She leaned against the workbench and closed one eye. "As for my idea, it's probably not anywhere near as good as what you'll be doing. I mean, you're an *artisan*. I worked on the principle that the best way to hide something was to put it right out in plain sight where it's so obvious that nobody really *sees* it. You understand?"

Caspar nodded. "Your principle is most sound. But with the secret compartment, this is not always easy to do. You have seen other desks by Riesener? The mechanisms and compartments are always most complicated."

"I know. But my idea takes a whole different approach."

Caspar smiled tolerantly. "Then tell me, by all means. I promise to think about it."

Wren explained.

Sixteen

Gently, sweetly, the Christmas season settled over France like softly falling snow.

Mercifully, wars and the rumors of war seemed to subside. Frenchmen planned their traditional family dinners, hummed the old carols, and hid gifts for the children under the bed.

It was just about then that a minor news item, reported with relish on the French national radio, captured the heart of the country. It was a simple story, one that might well have been ignored in other, less amiable seasons. But a Christmas season reference caught the eye of an alert news editor, who picked it up and added it to his nightly news report. The story was brief:

A long-lost love letter from Marie Antoinette to the king has been discovered by two young American scholars now visiting France. Mr. Nicholas Otter and Miss Wren Wooding, graduates of Harvard University, have declined to reveal the exact contents. "The letter contains a line or two of very intimate, very romantic language, as part of a Christmas greeting. We thought it best not to quote it, but it is very clear that the king must have had a very joyous and pleasant Christmas in 1772," said Mr. Otter, smiling.

Alas, the announcer added, with the mock-regret that is so typically French, what a pity that the best part cannot be repeated on the air!

France smiled. Papa winked, and Maman shot him a warning glance. Too late. The children, of course, raised insistent questions at once.

So did the editors of virtually all of the major newspapers throughout the country.

As all the world knows, the French are a stubbornly practical nation. Though it is well concealed, it cannot be denied that a strain of the romantic runs deep in them; if one is very careful not to try to manage their hearts, they will give them freely. Because editors are paid to know such things, assignments were issued at once:

These two young Americans are in Paris. Find them.
Get the full text of this letter.
Show it to our legal staff. Can we print it?
Find out if they want to sell it.
For how much?
Should we buy their exclusive story?

"Je-zuzz," said Wren, "look at that mob!"

Their cab inched its way along the Rue St. Honoré and rolled to a cautious stop before the entrance of the Hotel France et Choiseul. Within seconds it was ringed by clamoring reporters. Microphones were thrust into the car's open window, while cameras zoomed in to register the startled faces of Nicholas Otter and Wren Wooding.

They paid the driver and moved with the greatest of difficulty through the press of reporters and on into the open central court of the hotel. There Nicholas mounted the steps leading to the manager's office, turned, and lifted his hand. Silence fell at once.

"Gentlemen . . . and . . . uh . . . ladies of the press. I know you are here to talk to us about the letter we found. May we be excused for an hour or two, so that we may prepare a written statement and—"

A furor greeted these words at once. A written statement, it seemed, was thoroughly unacceptable.

"We understand the English," a reporter called out. Heads nodded everywhere. "We wish to see this letter. The readers of our magazine wish to see it. *Paris-Match* is willing to discuss an arrangement—"

An outcry of protest shouted the speaker down. "Arrangements," it seemed, were widely available. Attracted to the scene, guests of the hotel were now drifting from the bar and lounge. Hotel staff, trailing mops and brooms, joined the throng. From the street outside, passersby peered in.

"Okay, P. T. Barnum," whispered Wren, "the rubes are outside the tent. Now what do you do?"

"Damn if I know," hissed Nicholas. "I planted a little story so maybe one or two reporters might pick it up. But look at this. It's crazy."

"*Mr. Otter!*" The short figure of a man moved easily through the crowd, which made way for him respectfully. Here, it seemed, was a major force. "Permit me to introduce myself, Mr. Otter." He raised his hat an inch and bowed. "I am Jean-Paul Bart, representing our national television. On behalf of my colleagues, may I offer the small suggestion? Let us do as you say—" He held up a hand at the murmur of protest. "Let us do as you say, I repeat. Let us hear this written statement. But also, Mr. Otter, let us have the open forum. Let us ask you our questions. You will show us the intriguing letter, I think, because you must, no? If we do not see it, it may not exist. We must be sure, Mr. Otter, that this is no deception. You understand?"

"A press conference, you mean?" said Nicholas.

"Exactly, sir."

Nicholas nodded slowly. "Yes, what you say is fair and reasonable, Mr. Bart. In an hour or two, as I said, we will have a written statement. And we will answer your questions, if we can."

"For publication, Mr. Otter. Nothing off-the-record, as with some of your political spokesmen." The crowd of journalists growled their approval.

"Absolutely," said Nicholas. "We have no reason to want it any other way."

"Then it is agreed," said Bart. He looked at his watch. "It is now one o'clock. Shall we say the main lounge, at three?"

Wren closed the door and locked it carefully.

"This gets more complicated," she said tautly. "You never said anything about press conferences. A nice, quiet little story, you told me. Just the way you and the professor worked it out. A small mention, to confirm the thing publicly, so Gilliat's could be told about it. You and your nice, quiet little story. Did you see that mob down there? If only half of them write this up, we'll be under every microscope in the world. I think I'm getting nervous again."

Nicholas picked up the telephone.

"Room Twenty-eight," he said. "*Vingt-huit, s'il vous plaît.*" He stared at the floor, waiting, his face blank. "Hel-lo? Father Pierre? We're in our room now. Will you join us? We're in Room Twenty-one. Right."

"That's another thing," said Wren. "More wrinkles. You said we'd have a nice, simple crime . . ." Nicholas rose and went to the door. Almost at once there was a soft knock. He opened it quickly, and Planchet, gowned in the anonymous habit of a parish priest, slipped in, smiling gently.

"Bless you, my children," he murmured.

Precisely at three, flanked by Wren and "Father Pierre," Nicholas strode into the lounge of the hotel, a sheet of paper in one hand, his briefcase in the other. The room was packed with reporters, an assortment of guests, and hotel staff. Nicholas led the way through the crowd to the small raised platform near the bar and mounted it.

"Thank you for your patience and your courtesy," he said quietly. "With your permission, I will first read the statement we have prepared. Thereafter, I will do my best to answer your questions. Our statement says this: Miss Wooding and I hold degrees in art history from Harvard University. We came to France to work on a book about the great French classical painters."

A murmur of pleased surprise ran through the room. Nicholas waited for the sound to die down, then continued.

"In our travels through France we were fortunate enough to meet Father Pierre. He stands with me today. As guests in his home we admired an old table in his entry hall . . . and offered to purchase it. This old table has been in Father Pierre's family for many, many years. He remembers it from his childhood and has told me that his father remembered it when *he* was a child. We agreed on the price and had the table shipped back to Paris, then con-

tinued our travels. When we returned to Paris, we had time
to examine the old table carefully.

"We discovered a letter in a cleverly concealed secret
compartment in the beautiful inlaid surface. We now have
reason to believe that this desk may have been a Christmas
gift given to Louis XVI by his wife, Marie Antoinette. We
also have reason to believe that the desk was the work of
Jean-Henri Riesener. The queen's letter is quite brief—no
more than a note, in fact. It consists of seventy words,
twenty-four of which have a strongly erotic significance
and which—with Father Pierre's advice to guide us—we
have decided not to make public."

Nicholas paused and looked up, smiling diffidently. "If I
may depart from my prepared statement, it is well known
that scholarly papers are not widely read by young children. It is our intention to reveal the full transcript of this
letter in a paper that we hope will appear in the scholarly
press. But to continue. The portion of the letter that I can
reveal says this:

> My heart,
> It is the time of year for the giving of gifts to those we
> love, and this little writing table is yours, from me. Riesen-
> er, as always, has added our secret drawer. Hide this there.

Nicholas paused again. "From this point I will omit the
explicit text. The note then says, 'Before God, I swear that
you . . .' followed by a few more words we must omit. It
closes simply, saying, 'Yours forever, Marie Antoinette.'"

Nicholas folded the paper and placed it carefully in his
pocket.

The silence that had held the room attentive seemed
now to deepen. For a brief moment the tenderness of the
long-dead queen for her husband seemed to touch them

all. Here and there a few reporters shifted uneasily from foot to foot, as though uncertain where to start.

"*Young man!*" a crisp voice—obviously American— snapped sharply from the back of the room. Heads swiveled suddenly to see who it was who had broken the spell.

"Sir?" said Nicholas politely.

"This letter is doubtless interesting to the members of the press. But are you seriously suggesting that you and your friend have discovered an original Riesener writing table? Are you aware that there are only four authenticated tables by Riesener in the world? I must say, regretfully, that I am forced to doubt it—until and unless I can see it for myself!"

Jean-Paul Bart turned his attention back to Nicholas, his face pink with excitement. "Do you recognize who it is who challenges you, Mr. Otter? It is your own countryman, Lewis Poe Tewksbury!"

Heads craned, and the room buzzed with conversation.

"Yes, Mr. Otter," said Bart, faint mockery in his tone, "a world-famous expert in these matters. And you? What do you now say, sir?"

"I know of the reputation of Professor Tewksbury, of course," said Nicholas. "Although retired, he is one of the great men of Harvard University." Nicholas paused, as though to collect his thoughts. "If Professor Tewksbury wishes to see the desk, we would be honored. We consent, at once and gladly." A small spatter of applause greeted these words. Nicholas held up his hand. "It occurs to me that since Professor Tewksbury is not a member of the press, we would be happy to allow *him* to study the full text of the letter. We ask only that he agree not to reveal the exact language."

Bart turned to the professor. "We ask you to do so, please, sir. You may verify its authenticity, perhaps."

Tewksbury frowned doubtfully. "To read this letter, Mr.

Bart, will be of little assistance to you and your colleagues. I would have to confer with your own experts. The paper would have to be tested most carefully. Inks would have to be analyzed, and calligraphy, grammar . . ." The professor raised his hands helplessly. "It is most technical, I assure you. In any case, I am here in Paris to do research on my own new book. I have no time for these matters. I wish only to remind you again that it is the writing table that is the far more important matter, sir."

"To scholars and collectors, yes," said Bart. "But it is the letter that most interests the people of France. Would you at least look at it . . . informally?"

Professor Tewksbury shrugged. "Very well, if you insist. You will understand that I cannot authenticate it." He walked purposefully to the front of the room, fishing in his pocket for his silvery spectacles. Nicholas dipped into his briefcase and carefully extracted a stiff folder of red leather. The reporters, crowding close, had only the barest glimpse of a small sheet of paper, tinted by age to a creamy ivory. He handed the folder to the professor, who read it at once. Then, after staring thoughtfully at the ceiling, Tewksbury read it again, closed the folder, and handed it back to Nicholas.

"Well, sir," said Bart. "What do you think?"

"I have already said that a firm opinion at this point would be utterly without meaning. It may be genuine. It may not. The language is correct; also the grammar. The salutation is one the queen used many, many times. But be careful, gentlemen! These things may also be forged."

"Your caution is commendable, no doubt," said Bart dryly. "But what of the words that Mr. Otter will not reveal? Eh?"

Professor Tewksbury's cheeks reddened slightly.

"Genuine or not, the content of these lines might best be left unspoken. Let me say this. The queen speaks of certain intimate aspects of sexual activity. Quite specifically. In this matter I agree with Mr. Otter and the clergyman; it would probably be best not to reveal it to the general public and the press. But I repeat, it is the writing table that should be the issue here. If it is genuine, then the letter is most likely also genuine. If it is not, then the letter is simply a clever forgery!"

The old man had allowed an edge of hostility to creep into his voice, listening to the murmur of resentment without expression. A brief moment of silence fell, and Jean-Paul Bart seized the opening and moved swiftly to fill it.

"Professor Tewksbury," he called. "Would you agree that a panel of experts is needed to authenticate this letter . . . and this desk you appear to doubt so vigorously?"

"I do not doubt, and I do not accept," said the professor acidly. "But, yes. I would agree. A panel of experts is exactly what is needed."

"And would you agree to be a member of that panel?" said Bart softly.

"If the experts are of sufficient stature, yes," said Tewksbury.

"Aristide Duclos of the Louvre, perhaps," purred Bart.

"Dr. Duclos? Of course. I have the greatest respect for Dr. Duclos."

"And—let me see—François Varenne, perhaps? The famous dealer and connoisseur? What of him?"

"Equally, an excellent man," said the professor. "If you can persuade them."

"But naturally," said Bart. "If I can persuade them. But I may say to them that Lewis Poe Tewksbury is also willing, yes?"

"Yes," said Tewksbury firmly.

"Ex-cellent!" cried Bart. "And I shall arrange for this panel to meet on my Friday program!"

"On . . . on television, you mean?" said the professor.

"On television," said Bart triumphantly. "Until then, I suggest that no more questions be asked, if you please."

The roar of protest from the assembled reporters was almost deafening.

Wren nudged Nicholas. "Fifty million Frenchmen can't be right." She frowned. "Can they?"

Seventeen

"Today's newspaper reports of our press conference agree on at least one thing," said the professor happily. "I am the villain. You two are the heroes."

"Look at this," grumbled Planchet. "Pictures in every paper, and only *L'Humanité* shows my face! One can hardly make me out."

"It happens to be a damn lucky break, too," said Wren. "After all, you live in Brussels, but you do business in Paris, and the one thing we don't need is a good clear picture of *you.*"

"I like *Le Figaro*'s story best, I think," said the professor. "They praise the politeness of Mr. Otter, the modesty of Miss Wooding, while bitterly attacking that sour old man Professor Tewksbury. They've decided that I have attacked France itself. And of course what they have done is to create an acknowledgment that these nice young people have made an important discovery, and the mean old skeptic is obviously blinded by jealousy."

"This book we're supposed to be writing made a lot of points, too," said Nicholas. "In fact, maybe we ought to write the damn thing. *Le Monde* mentions it prominently. So does *France-Soir* and *L'Aurore*. After all, it's a book that defends the traditional art of France—and who the hell can be against *that*?"

"The book was good, and the professor was good, but it was kindly old Father Pierre here who carried the day," said Wren. "All he had to do was stand up there, oozing piety. You gave out a kind of holy glow, Planchet. You really did."

"Thank you," said Pierre. "I am forced to agree. The strange thing is that when a man puts on this black garment and hangs a simple wooden cross around his neck, it creates a certain feeling of goodness." He smiled shyly. "It is not logical, of course."

"On the contrary," said Nicholas. "I know you to be a man of mercy. When you tapped me on the head with that hammer, you could have broken my damn skull open. Instead, you gave me a walnut and put me to sleep. I've been meaning to thank you for that, as a matter of fact."

"Anyway," said Wren, "we got our favorable newspaper stories today, and we go on network television tonight. I'm trying to decide what to wear."

"What's wrong with what you've got on?" said Nicholas. "You look fine."

"Jeans?" Wren was outraged. "Paris happens to be the fashion capital of the world, rockhead. I've got time to find me a long skirt, maybe, and a simple little sleeveless blouse—maybe a metallic, so it shimmers when I inhale. Light makeup, simple pumps, no handbag—what d'you think?"

"You'll look like the lead singer for a failed rock group,"

said Nicholas. "We're poor but honest art scholars, remember? You wear the denims. Denims are basic American. Broom the sequins, and that's an order."

"Planchet gets to dress up," complained Wren. "Even the professor gets to carry his cane. You guys have all the fun, and I come out looking like somebody's retarded cousin. Some gang."

Nicholas stooped to pick up the newspapers that lay on the floor. "You hang tough, kid, and I'll drown you in gowns by Givenchy. For now—blue jeans. Now, help me get all the newspapers put together. We'll need them in New York."

Planchet rose and made the sign of the cross. "And I must disappear, my children. As we have agreed. You have my address in Brussels?"

Tewksbury patted his pocket. "Safe and sound, Pierre. You'll be careful about spending the money? You'll follow the plan in disposing of your clerical habit?"

"The money goes to sleep in a little box for one year, yes. As for these clothes—a priest enters the *pissoir* at the Gare du Nord carrying his small valise; a quietly dressed man of business comes out carrying the same valise. The garment I will myself burn when I arrive at my home. A short career in the Church, my friends, but a profitable one." Planchet shook hands with Nicholas and the professor, bowed minutely to Wren, and took his leave.

"How much?" said Wren after a brief pause.

"Three thousand dollars," said Nicholas, "and damn cheap at the price."

"I'd say so," said Wren. "Where else can you buy a whole religious order for three thousand dollars?"

"It's time for me to go, too," said Tewksbury. "It won't do for us to be discovered together, you know. We're sworn opponents at the moment."

"You did a fantastic acting job yesterday, professor," said

Wren. "I didn't know you had it in you. I mean, I knew what was going on, and you had *me* irritated. Where did you learn to be so nasty?"

"Faculty meetings, my dear."

"Keep it up, sir. You'll have to be just as nasty on to-night's television thing," said Nicholas.

Tewksbury nodded. "Yes. I'm going to cut you two up into small pieces." His tone had flattened suddenly, and he sounded prim and unpleasant. Unexpectedly, he winked.

"Show biz," said Wren, "is a tough racket. It's a jungle out there, you know?"

The television studio seemed as spacious as a cathedral, and nearly as quiet. Studio B, the receptionist had said; they opened the door and peered in.

Far across the floor, three cameras dominated the scene. Dark and unattended, they sat on little wheeled platforms. Thick black cables were everywhere, twined like a nest of snakes and connected to sockets set in the floor. Overhead, thin structural girders were studded with row upon row of lights, each flapped at the sides with metal fins.

The set itself seemed almost an afterthought. It sat against a gray-curtain backdrop and consisted of a desk flanked by two comfortable-looking couches. Directly above these, microphones were suspended on angled booms.

The control room, behind a large tilted pane of glass, was positioned to the right of the set. Through the glass Wren could see figures of men seated at various control panels.

"Where do people sit? I mean . . . no chairs?" whispered Wren.

"No studio audience," said Nicholas. "Just the crew."

"What do we do? Wait to be noticed?"

As though on cue, the door to the control room opened and a young man came down the steps quickly and walked toward them, smiling. He carried a clipboard with a tiny, hooded light at the top.

"You will be Mr. Otter and Miss Wooding, no doubt. How good of you to come so early. I am Gaby Magsino, the director of this weekly masterpiece!" He shook hands with them. "We have forty minutes to air time, nearly. Where would you like to wait? We have the special room for our guests. Or Miss Wooding would like to see our control room?"

"We came early because we rode in the truck with the writing table," said Nicholas. "They took it to the platform behind the building, but they wouldn't let us in. We'd like to make sure it's safe, if it's possible."

Magsino slapped his forehead lightly. "How stupid of me! But of course. I could not come to meet you at once because I was on the telephone. They called me, and I have asked them to bring your table here, to the set. It must be here by now. Come. I will show you."

He walked across the floor to the curtain, slipping between the overlap of its center sections, Nicholas and Wren at his heels. The writing table had already been delivered. It sat by the door in a corner, covered with the sheet borrowed from the hotel.

"How mysterious it looks," said Magsino. He ran a hand through his closely cropped black hair. "It gives me an idea. Let us bring it on camera covered just so. Let us *keep* it covered for the first part of your discussion, so that our audience will grow more and more curious to see it, yes? Then, when the experts are ready, we remove the cloth! I like it. The element of suspense, you see?"

"I like you," said Wren. "You are absolutely the first person who isn't all uptight about our table. And I like your idea."

Magsino grinned. "Do not be deceived by my charming manner, Miss Wooding. I don't give a damn if your desk is a fraud. It will make a good story. I don't care if it is genuine. It will also make a good story. As to what the experts decide, for me it is a matter of indifference. I hope you understand."

"I do, I do," said Wren. "Heads you win, tails you win. One more thing, Mr. Magsino. How about the way I'm dressed? Too informal?"

"Not at all," said the director promptly. "Dresses are a disaster on camera. Women cross their legs, and the audience always stops listening to take a peek. It breaks up the segment all the time."

"What's a segment?" said Wren.

"Why, a portion of the program, of course," said Magsino. "You have never seen *Evening Report*? It is much like your interview programs in the United States. We usually have four guests. Each guest is . . . a segment. Tonight . . ." He lifted a sheet on the clipboard. "Tonight we have the minister of education and the head of the teachers' union. They are the first segment. Twelve minutes. Then we change the pace. Amalia Rodrigues—very beautiful, very Portuguese—will sing the Fada music. This is the second segment. Also twelve minutes. Then . . . our climax!" Nicholas and Wren leaned forward.

"In segment three we will have two male homosexuals and two lesbians. They will discuss the New Morality! It will be a sensation; nothing like it has ever been done in France on television! Twenty-four minutes—the highlight of the program!"

"Then us," said Wren faintly.

"Exactly. Segment four—twelve minutes. Your mysterious table—the long-lost love letter! Marvelous!"

"We follow a matched set of fruits and nuts?" said Wren.

"It's just fine, Mr. Magsino," said Nicholas calmly. "We know nothing about television. You do. We are in your hands."

"How gracious of you, Mr. Otter. It is the very impression I felt when I read about you in the newspapers this morning. You must only be natural, and all will go well." He glanced hurriedly at his watch. "I must leave you now. You may stay here, near your table, if you wish. Please try not to cough, once we are on the air, yes?"

Wren waited until he was well out of earshot.

"Homos and dikes," she said in a hollow voice. "Are you sure Barbara Walters started this way?"

Jean-Paul Bart turned on a hand cue from the floor director and smiled into Camera Two.

"And now, ladies and gentlemen, we come to the final portion of my *Evening Report*. A long-lost letter—is it a fraud? Or genuine? What did Marie Antoinette write that is too naughty for us to hear? Let me begin by reading that part of the letter that has been approved for general consumption."

While Bart read from the letter, Nicholas and Wren walked softly in from one side of the set, out of the camera's range, and seated themselves on the couch on the left. Opposite them, on the other side of Bart's desk, Tewksbury, Dr. Duclos, and Varenne arranged themselves on the empty couch.

" With me in the studio tonight is the young couple who discovered this letter in a very old desk. Miss Wren Wooding and Mr. Nicholas Otter." Camera One, already in position, zoomed in as they dipped their heads self-consciously.

"To question them about this startling discovery, I have invited three world-famous experts to join us tonight. Professor Lewis Tewksbury, the noted Harvard professor, now retired. Dr. Aristide Duclos, associate curator and head of the Antiquarian Department of the Louvre. And the famous collector and dealer Mr. François Varenne. Miss Wooding and Mr. Otter speak French, and you may question them directly. I will add a question or two here and there, hm?" Bart preened himself briefly and turned to the experts. "Gentlemen, who will begin the questioning?"

Tewksbury spoke up at once, effectively riding over the tentative words that hung on Varenne's lips.

"Utter nonsense!" he grated. "I am offended to find myself party to this affair. A matter of serious and substantial scholarship is involved, Mr. Bart. Authentication of this letter—or the desk in which it was found—is a matter of weeks and weeks of painstaking examination and testing. There are less than fifteen minutes remaining in this program, sir!"

"But you did agree to appear," said Bart smoothly.

"For general discussion—yes. But you failed to tell me that—"

"A moment, please, professor," said Duclos. "Let us have more light and less heat, please. What Professor Tewksbury has said is quite true, Mr. Bart. Authentication by scientific tests can take weeks, or even months. I defer to the professor's opinion in this . . . and it agrees also with my own experience at the Louvre. On the other hand . . ." He paused, searching for words.

"On the other hand, I must say candidly that human judgment remains the final determinant, sir. In this, I think the learned professor will also agree."

Tewksbury stared straight ahead.

"And Mr. Varenne," said Bart. "What does *he* say?"

François Varenne puffed calmly on his pipe. "I agree with both of my distinguished colleagues. Tests are useful—as an aid to judgment. But they are not a substitute for judgment, Mr. Bart. The true *looks* true, sir. It has the integrity of line, the fidelity to detail, the sense of wholeness, of *soul*—and technology cannot measure such things, in my experience."

"Therefore, you are willing to look at this letter—and the desk—and give us your opinion tonight?"

"My preliminary opinion, yes," said Varenne.

Turning to Nicholas, Bart said, "Will you please show Mr. Varenne the letter from Marie Antoinette?"

Slowly Nicholas extracted the red leather folder from his briefcase, the zoom lens of the camera in tight on his hands. "Please explain to your audience why the whole letter cannot be read aloud," he said. While Bart conveyed this to his audience, Nicholas rose and brought the letter to Varenne, who examined it front and back, then read it slowly and carefully, smiling here and there.

"This letter . . . is genuine. Or it is a superlative copy," said Varenne. "I agree with Mr. Otter, however, that it should not be read aloud." He offered the letter to Tewksbury, who shook his head disdainfully, then passed it to Duclos.

The museum official first held the paper up to the light and studied it carefully. Then, from an inside pocket of his coat he took a small magnifying glass and bent over the text of the letter, studying it with painstaking care. When his examination had been completed, Duclos shrugged.

"The paper? Yes, the paper is right. Or it looks right. Chemical tests are needed, in my opinion. The style of writing and the grammar also look right. The letter, therefore looks genuine. For the moment, that is all I can say with assurance."

Nicholas retrieved the letter and returned to his seat. Bart lifted a finger, commanding attention. "May I take it, then, that not one of our experts will say that the letter from Marie Antoinette is a forgery? That, in fact, it may be genuine?"

"Why do you waste time on this letter?" said Tewksbury sarcastically. "It is the desk we should be looking at, not the letter! Why do you keep it covered? What are you trying to conceal?"

"Mr. Otter?" said Bart.

Nicholas rose once again and walked toward the cameras. The writing table, sitting directly in the center of the set, was still covered with the sheet. Nicholas pulled it away and stood to one side. Duclos sprang to his feet, his eyes shining.

"Incredible!" he breathed. "We have the sister to this masterpiece in our museum!" He walked to the table, followed by Varenne, and the two men circled the desk slowly, in opposite directions. As for the writing table, under the lights it glowed and shimmered, its delicate proportions and elegance clearly manifest.

"The table is genuine," said Varenne flatly. "Now you may see what I mean. It has the soul. One need only see it to know. The technical details combine to produce a true work of art. I'm sure of it. It will pass every test, but it needs no tests. It speaks for itself."

"It is a fantastic find," cried Duclos. He darted to Nicholas and Wren, to shake their hands solemnly. "You have saved a treasure, and I thank you, just as all France will thank you!"

"Did you notice the left-front leg?" said Wren. "There's something funny about it. I never noticed it in ordinary light. But the lights in the studio are incredibly bright." She paused. "If you look very close, I think you can see it." She knelt down by the leg of the desk, pointing with her finger, while the cameras rolled in very close. "Here. This little dark harline? It's not on the other leg." Her fingernail traced along the crack.

"Yes," said Duclos. "I see what you mean!" He extended his finger and probed gently. Promptly, the front face of the leg swung open, like a tall and narrow door, and a cascade of diamonds, emeralds, rubies, and pearls tumbled out of the compact little cavity onto the studio floor.

"Well, sir," said Bart, "what do you make of this?"

"I'm flabbergasted," said Professor Tewksbury. "Absolutely flabbergasted. The gems seem genuine. Who can tell why they were hidden away? And if the gems are genuine—"

"They *are*, professor," said Duclos, dropping a jeweler's loupe from his eye. "If the gems are genuine, the letter is genuine. If the letter is genuine, the table is genuine. If I, Aristide Duclos, am asked for my opinion, that is it!"

Delighted with his coup, Jean-Paul Bart brought the program to a graceful close, Wren returned to the couch and sat quietly next to Nicholas, while the red lights of the cameras were turned off and the lights overhead, one by one, were cut.

"Listen," said Nicholas, "where the hell—"

"Otch-way the ikes-may," said Wren softly.

"Holy it-shay," mumbled Nicholas.

Eighteen

"The facts are simple," said Roland Swain. "I can find no evidence that Carl Becker exists. None of my people have heard of him. *I* have not heard of him. On the basis of all this, what might one logically conclude, Peel?"

"A fig-a-ment of the imagination, I'd say," said Peel, "and therefore, some trick by that old man and those two young Americans. That would be my guess, Mr. Swain."

"And mine, Peel, and mine. Now, let us set some more facts out on the table. Every major French newspaper carries a story—most of them on the front page, mind you—about the Marie Antoinette letter. Every one, Peel! Paris, Marseilles, Lyons, Strasbourg, Nantes . . ." Swain nudged the stack of papers restlessly. "Would you say that an old man and two young assistants could produce that kind of press, Peel?"

Peel shook his head.

"No more would I, Peel. To that, add coverage on French national radio and a guest appearance on the most popular interview program on French television! These are *facts,* Peel."

"I know," said Peel. "The reports came straight to me, didn't they, sir?"

"And now, the final fact," said Swain. "These three Americans have somehow managed to produce firm authentication from Aristide Duclos of the Louvre and that pompous ass François Varenne. Duclos, no less! It staggers me to think of what kind of power was needed to achieve this. Despite all the evidence to the contrary, I am therefore forced to the reluctant conclusion that Carl Becker *does* exist, Peel!"

Peel struggled with a new thought. "Look here, Mr. Swain. Maybe this Carl Becker name is just a *fake* name. See what I mean? There *is* a Carl Becker, but he isn't *called* Carl Becker. Like you gave Caspar this Van der Ek name, instead of calling him by his real name, Planchet, I mean."

"Yes, yes," said Swain wearily, "I followed the same line in my investigations. All to no avail. Whether he's called Carl Becker, or whether he's called something else, the fact remains. He's strong enough to plant an authentication that will help to sell that blasted desk. Gilliat's will take it on. Some rich collector or some museum will buy it, and my share will be a pittance! It's infuriating."

"Hang on a bit," said Peel. "I've just had another thought. Maybe we've been going at this the wrong way 'round, sir."

"Really," said Swain, his tone frosted. "And what might be the *right* way 'round, Peel?"

"Well, sir. Maybe we've been kidnapping the wrong parties. We took that Miss Wooding, sir, and it turned about and bit back, believe you me. Now, didn't it, sir?"

Swain nodded.

"But, I say to myself, what's this Carl Becker thinking right about now? His Professor Tewksbury and his Nicholas Otter and his Miss Wooding have all gone and done a bunk on him, right? Pulled out and gone independent, they have, sir."

"Get to it, man. You're running in a circle."

"The *desk*, Mr. Swain. That's what we ought to be kidnapping, sir, the desk! Once we get our hands on that blinking desk, we'll flush Mr. Carl Becker out of the bushes, right enough. You may not have heard of him, sir. But he'll have heard of *you*, if you see what I mean."

"And he'll get in touch with me," drawled Swain. "Mr. Peel, you have put your finger on a most compelling point! What an elegant inspiration! Of course. We shall kidnap the desk."

"The trouble is," said Peel, "that I don't know where it is. Right at the moment, I mean." He frowned. "I don't even know where to start looking, sir."

"As to that, Peel, you need have no worry. *I* know where it is, and we shall pack our bags and purchase our tickets tomorrow morning."

Peel's frown dissolved. "And where are we off to, Mr. Swain? If you don't mind my asking, I mean."

"Not at all, Peel, not at all. We're off for New York and Boston, my lad."

"The Yew Ess of Aye, is it? Well, well. I've never been there, Mr. Swain!" Peel rubbed his neck thoughtfully. "I might even get a chance to chat a bit with that Miss Wooding. There's a few things I'd like to say to her, and that's the god's truth, sir."

Nineteen

"Goddamn," said Wren, "but it's good to be at home. I went out right after you left and bought you some mops and brushes and a wild polka-dot dustpan. They came out with a new kind of potato chip while we were gone, too. Sort of like engineered ersatz—shaped like one of those funny Salvador Dali watches. Fantastic country. I tell you, Nicholas, it's a pleasure to wash my hair in real American water. It's got all those chemicals in it, and I swear they're better for hair than they are for teeth."

She flopped into the easy chair and sighed luxuriously. "You look good to me, too. We ought to go to bed. We've been so damn busy, all the trend lines are down."

"I can't find my coin," said Nicholas. "I definitely remember locking that Becker in my metal box and sticking it under my shirts. It's gone."

"Look in my old bathing suit; top shelf, clothes closet. I

took the Becker out of your dumb box. It's the first thing crooks look for. Where have you been, anyway?"

"Tewksbury's. Strategy meeting. And guess who called? Mr. Harold Gilliat himself. President of Gilliat's."

Wren sat up straighter. "No less. What did he want?"

Nicholas grinned. "He wondered if Tewksbury knew how to get in touch with us. He wants to make the desk the main piece in their next Evening Sale. Next month. He thought the desk, the jewels, and the letter could be sold together. All three to one bidder."

"Wow. What did the professor say?"

"He's incredible. He kept saying that he had no authority to speak for us, that he wasn't connected to us in any way. He said Gilliat's ought to call in more experts, and Harold Gilliat said that Duclos and Varenne were plenty good enough for him. Anyway, Tewksbury is supposed to call us, and we're supposed to call Gilliat and go down to New York and talk things over. But hang on a minute. I want to get that Becker." He rummaged in the closet briefly and emerged with the bathing suit, rolled into a ball.

"Got it," he said happily.

"Listen," said Wren, "*do* we sell all three of the things, or not? What do you think?"

"Gilliat says yes. He thinks there's maybe eight hundred thousand in the whole package. When Tewksbury relayed that one, I damn near fell off the chair." Nicholas shook his head. "Eight hundred thousand dollars. I bet you could buy a third interest in Poland for eight hundred thousand dollars."

"It's funny," said Wren reflectively. "When I had those old clocks and coins, I felt richer."

"Right," said Nicholas. "You give me a roll of fifty-cent pieces; that's *money*." He flipped the golden Becker into the air and caught it deftly. "Heads it is. We call Gilliat and set up a date."

"What if it had come up tails?"

"We call Gilliat and set up a date." He gave his eyebrows a Groucho wiggle. "Like I say. With this coin, I feel lucky."

"Hand me some of those engineered potato chips, will you, Admiral? I think there's an aphrodisiac in these things."

Nicholas tossed her the box and reached for the phone.

The oaken door marked "President" swung open, and Harold Gilliat poked his head out and waved a beckoning hand.

"Nick Otter? Wren Wooding? Sorry to keep you waiting. C'mon in, c'mon in!"

He spoke with animation and assurance, holding the door to his inner office wide to give them room to pass. He was tall and thin, with a remarkable head of wavy black hair, and dark brown eyes set off by a complexion so dark he seemed almost Arabic.

"You look like an Arab," said Wren.

Harold Gilliat's teeth flashed white in a wide smile. "You're telling me," he said. "Everyone says I look like the president of Egypt. Sadat? Can you see it?" He turned his face to profile. "You have to imagine the mustache."

The walls of the office were hung with hundreds of framed photographs, virtually all of proud owners standing by their acquisitions, shaking hands with Harold Gilliat. A large executive desk sat to one side, two small chairs facing it. On the opposite side of the office a leather sofa and three easy chairs had been grouped around a low round table. A magnificent Persian rug covered the floor from wall to wall.

"How did you get to be president?" said Wren. "You're not even wearing a tie, and your jacket doesn't match your pants. This is such a stuffy place, full of Republicans and people who still think Nixon got a tough break. You don't fit. In fact, you even look like a Democrat."

"If you're a Democrat, I'm a Democrat," said Gilliat. "On the other hand, if you're a Republican, I'm a Republican. *That's* how I got to be president." He waved them to the easy chairs. "C'mon. Let's get comfortable." He sank onto the sofa and stretched. "I've got five uncles and five aunts, see? They held the stock. I mean *all* the stock. Some· of them were so conservative they didn't trust Barry Goldwater. With them I didn't trust Barry Goldwater, either. Then there was the *liberal* side of the family. They liked Jack Kennedy, mostly. So I liked Jack Kennedy. After twelve years of this, I had their proxies. I was thirty-one when I started. Twelve years later I was eighty-eight. I felt eighty-eight, anyway. But I had the proxies, and in a few more years I was president, and a few years after that, I had the stock, too. Damn good thing. I've got nine cousins and two brothers and a sister—all very blond, with good backhands. Most of them sit around counting up the inches they get in the society pages of the New York *Times.* They never think about money, and I never think about anything else. Get the picture?"

"You really open up," said Wren. "I'm impressed."

"I'm setting you up," said Gilliat, grinning. "I want you to think that way when we get to the crunch."

"What crunch?" said Wren.

"Ask Nick, here. He sits like a blotter, sopping up all the ink and saying nothing. He's doing what I'm doing. Trying to get his guns in position for the negotiating. Right, Nick?"

"We had a call from Professor Tewksbury," said Nicholas carefully. "He said you wanted to talk to us about selling the writing table."

"Correcto," said Gilliat. "Housekeeping stuff, mostly. Terms of sale, reserve price, proof of ownership . . . and so on."

"*Correcto?*" said Wren. "Nobody talks like that, Mr. Gil-

liat, except maybe some characters in an F. Scott Fitz-
gerald."

Gilliat's president cocked his index finger at Wren and
flicked his thumb like a trigger. "You talk your funny way,
and I'll talk mine. It's a big dictionary; lots of words for ev-
erybody. Let's talk about the standard terms first. You familiar with them?"

"Not really," said Nicholas. "Why don't you fill us in?"

"Wilco." Gilliat lifted a sheet of paper from the table.
"This is it. I'll let you have it, but it's packed with legal gar-
bage, and practically impossible to understand. I'll boil it
down to the nuts and bolts. Okay?"

Nicholas nodded.

"First. We get ten percent on furniture if the stuff sells
for fifty thousand or more. You fit that one, in spades, dou-
bled and redoubled. Second. We get twelve and a half percent on jewelry, regardless of what it sells for. Third. We
get fifteen percent on books, manuscripts, engravings,
prints, and so on. Your letter fits that classification. Okay.
I'll take a flat ten percent on the whole thing, if you'll let us
put it all up for one package bid. Desk, jewels, letter; one
bid, ten percent. Got it?"

Nicholas nodded.

"Splendido," said Gilliat. Wren winced. "Fourth. You
can set your reserve price if you want to; it becomes the
price below which we cannot sell. Up to you. Our catalog
says that all bidders must assume that a reserve price has
been set on every item. Even if you do *not* set one. You follow?"

"I follow."

"It's fairly tricky. Set your reserve too low . . . and you
might have gotten more. Set it too high . . . and you
might not sell it at all. It can be an ouchie both ways, see?
That's one of the things I wanted to talk to you about. I'll

buy the whole package from you right now, and resell it as our own property."

"Je-zuzz," said Wren. "You're retail, too?"

"Professor Tewksbury said something about eight hundred thousand dollars," said Nicholas. "Is that what you'll pay us, or is that the reserve price you think we should set?"

"You ask hairy questions, Mr. Otter. Which reminds me. Why don't you call me Hank, and I'll call you Nick. Okay?"

"Mostly, I'd like a hairy answer."

"Six hundred thousand dollars," said Gilliat crisply. "I'll buy your package for six, after I see it. It might bring in eight at auction. That way, I'm up two. Or . . . I might get only five. It's been known to happen. So I'd be down one. But I do the sweating. You get the six, less *zero* commission, and while I sweat it out, you stay home and count the money. How does it sound?"

"I'll think about it," said Nicholas.

"Good answer. You could be president around here, too. I say that all the time, believe me. Okay, you think about it. I'll press on. Documents. I'll need your bill of sale, the export releases from customs, stuff like that. I can't move without it. It's the law. Understood?"

"Understood."

"Then, authentication. You have to know that we authenticate nothing for nobody. That's standard. We'll say, maybe, 'thought to be such-and-such' or 'authenticated by so-and-so.' But never by *us*, ever. Clear?"

Nicholas nodded.

"We handled some clocks and coins for you, so you know how we work. We've got our heads screwed on straight, and we think Shaw-Alcott is the best head auctioneer in town. If we have the time—and I hope we have—I'd like to put some four-color pictures of your desk in the catalog. It always adds some takeoff speed to the bidding when we do.

It's a nice frill." Gilliat lifted his hands, like a magician at the end of his act. "That's about it."

"Finito?" said Wren.

"Completo."

"Right," said Wren. "Then I have a question. When did you first decide that there's maybe one-million-two in this deal?"

Harold Gilliat's amiability dissolved instantly, to be replaced by a tightening of his mouth and a frown. He stared at Wren for a long moment, unblinking. "I must be losing my touch," he said slowly.

"C'mon, Hankerino," said Wren, "this cheeky routine may go down with your high-society rubes, but face it. You figured us all wrong. Christ almighty! We sat in your own goddamn auction room just a few months ago when Shaw-Alcott sold an Oeben-Riesener desk like ours for *six hundred and eighty thousand, four hundred and fifteen dollars.* Just the desk. No jewels. No letter from Marie Antoinette. And no opinions from Duclos and Varenne. If you're willing to pay six, then you must smell one million, two hundred thousand dollars. Up at Harvard they call it Math I. It's for freshmen."

Nicholas rose to his feet. "I'll tell you one thing, Mr. Gilliat. We might set a reserve—for the *desk.* If we do, I'm not sure for how much. I'll have to get back to you. As for the jewels and the letter, I have the feeling that we ought to hang on to them. I don't think they need to go up for auction at all. I think there's a private sale in this somewhere. But I said we'd think about what you've said, and we will."

"An answer today would be helpful," said Gilliat. "There's a lot to be done between now and the Evening Sale. After all, you two have the final say. Why not go somewhere and talk it over for an hour or so, and get back to me?"

"I've got a vote, Miss Wooding has a vote . . . and we have another partner." Wren shot a warning look at Nicholas. "Mr. Becker gets to vote, too," said Nicholas firmly. He . . . ah . . . he advises us."

"Becker. Becker. Somebody was asking me about a man named Becker. Not too long ago, either," said Gilliat. "I just can't place him."

"He used to be in swimwear," said Wren. "I don't care too much for him, frankly. But Nicholas here flips over him."

"I can see Central Park from my bedroom window," said Peel happily. "Uptown, they call it. And look at that, sir! A genuine garden hedge right here in the foyer! Would the Plaza Hotel be the very best in New York, Mr. Swain?"

"One of them, I suppose," said Swain idly. "Why?"

"I've never been in the best hotel anywhere," said Peel. "Never been in New York, neither, come to that. It's big, isn't it?"

"I daresay, Peel, I daresay. Nevertheless, Mr. Becker is here, and I'm going to find him. You're here to do a job of work. You'll do well to remember it."

"That I do, sir. But like I say, it's a big city. Where do I start?"

"The writing table must be in Boston now. It has to be; we've agreed on that. It's with young Otter or the old man. I want you to go up to Boston this morning, Mr. Peel, and take it. You'll hire a lorry and bring it back to me. Here."

"Here, sir? To the foyer?"

"To my room, Peel," said Swain patiently. "I've thought of a way to set a little trap to flush the mysterious Mr. Becker out into the open. The desk, Peel, shall be my bait. The time has come for Mr. Becker to deal with *me*. I mean to form a *combine*, Peel."

"Just as you say, Mr. Swain. It sounds very grand, sir.

But how do I get a desk into the hotel? I can't put it under my coat, now, can I?"

"You'll bring it along in the service lift, of course, nicely covered to protect it. I've spoken at some length to the manager; it's all arranged."

Peel scratched his head. "What must I do if Mr. Otter or the professor—whoever has it, I mean—won't give it up?"

"Yes, I've thought about that carefully. Here's exactly what you must do. When you get to Boston, you'll find a public telephone at the airport and one of those great, thick telephone books nearby, the ones with the yellow pages. We have the same sort of thing in England."

"So we do, sir."

"Find one of those books, Peel, and open it to M."

"M?"

"That's it. You are to call a moving company."

Peel looked blank.

"A company that moves furniture, Peel. It's called a moving company."

"Ahhh, *furniture removers,* sir!"

"Yes, but not under F, Peel. Under M—you'll be sure to remember?"

"Furniture removers . . . under M," said Peel, nodding.

"And when you choose one—any one will do—here's what I want you to say. . . ."

Professor Tewksbury opened the door. Two neatly uniformed moving men nodded pleasantly.

"Professor Lewis Tewksbury?" said the taller man. "We're from the Five Grossi Brothers." He gestured to the street, where a small van had been parked alongside the curb.

"Yes?" said Tewksbury. "What can I do for you, gentlemen?"

"We're here for the desk." He studied a sheet of paper. "The pickup order from my dispatcher says it's a . . . uh . . . a writing table." He handed the paper to Tewksbury, who waved it impatiently away. "I recall no such order," he said, backing slowly into the hall to close the door. "There must be—"

Alexander Peel, until then hidden by the wall beside the door, moved into view and slipped his foot into the doorway.

"It's like I told the lads here, professor. You can be a mite forgetful, isn't that right, sir? It was Mr. *Roland's* order, remember? Sends you his compliments, he does; and we're to take this desk right straight to New York. That's the message, professor, from Mr. Roland . . . *and the young lady.*"

"It's kinda cold out here, professor," said one of the moving men. "Is it okay if we step inside . . . or we can wait in the truck."

Helpless, Tewksbury gave way as Peel entered.

"Wait right here, will you, lads? The professor here and me need to chat a bit. Half a mo'—right?" Steering Tewksbury gently by the elbow, Peel moved down the center hall, peering casually into the rooms on each side. When they reached the parlor at the very end, he saw it. The *bureau du roi* sat just inside the door. Peel shook his head. That bloody Swain is a genius, he thought.

"Here we are, professor," he said cheerfully.

Tewksbury cast a despairing glance at the telephone, on its stand near the front entry.

"You'll want to hear about Miss Wooding," said Peel gently. There was the faintest shading of menace in his tone, and the old man sighed.

"Very well. After you, sir."

In the parlor, the other men now out of earshot, Peel continued to speak softly. "Mr. Swain sent me up here to pick up the desk. He wants to put it under—how did he put it?—under protective custody. That's what he wants me to tell you, sir. Under protective custody, just like Miss Wooding."

"You've taken Miss Wooding?" said the professor. "Is that how you found out where the desk was? You didn't torture her, did you, in God's name?"

"Never put a finger on her, professor. My word on it. Not that I didn't want to, mind. All we told her was that we'd take *you* unless she cooperated. That did the trick, I can tell you."

"Yes," said Tewksbury wearily, "so I see." He sighed. "Very well. Call your men and take it. Tell Swain that I've cooperated and that he can let Miss Wooding go. She's worth ten of the damn things."

Very shortly thereafter the van from the Five Grossi Brothers pulled away from the curb, the neatly covered desk in the back, Peel sitting calmly in front with the driver and his helper. Moodily, Lewis Tewksbury watched it roll down the street, turn a corner, and disappear. His mind busy with the implications of the newest turn of fortune, he turned angrily from the window. The small rug slid fractionally, and in an instant the old man, losing his balance, twisted frantically and fell in a heap to the floor.

"Damn, damn, *damn*," he said aloud. "I think I've broken my stupid ankle!"

Twenty

Nicholas Otter, orphaned at nine, hung up the phone and stared into space.

Lewis Poe Tewksbury, just a bare moment ago, had said he wanted to adopt him.

A father. Well, a stepfather, then. Old enough to be his grandfather, as a matter of fact. Still and all, a *father*.

"You've got the oddest expression on your face," said Wren. "That was Tewksbury who called, wasn't it? Is something wrong? If something is wrong, and if it's about that goddamn table, send me a memo, will you please? I'm up to here with it, and that's the truth."

"He's in the hospital," said Nicholas.

Shock washed across her face, followed by contrition. "Me and my mouth," said Wren. "I'm sorry, Nicholas, honest to god I am. What is it? Can we see him?" She went to the closet and pulled her coat from the hanger.

"Slow down, Redbird. He's broken his ankle; the right ankle. That's all. He says he slipped on a little rug in the front room. It's in a cast already. They'll discharge him tomorrow morning. Anyway, visiting hours are over for the day."

"Wow. You should have seen the expression on your face. I can't describe it. Like you were hit over the head or something."

"I felt that way. The professor was full of news. He says Peel came to the house to pay him a visit when we were in New York."

"*Peel?* Here in Boston? What the hell is Peel doing here?"

"As a matter of fact, he came to pick up the desk. Got it, too."

"*What?*"

"In broad daylight, says the professor. Assisted by the Five Grossi Brothers."

"The moving company? The ones who advertise on television?"

"*When you say move—we jump!* That's them." Nicholas shrugged. "Peel must have said 'move.'"

"Is that how the professor got hurt? I mean, did Peel push him around, or what?"

"It was pretty cute. Peel told the professor that you'd been kidnapped again. It sounded like Bruges all over again, so Tewksbury told them to take the thing. He slipped and fell after Peel was gone."

"If Peel is in Boston, can Swain be far behind?"

"My thought exactly," said Nicholas.

"No wonder you had that glassy-eyed look."

"No, it wasn't even that. It was something else the professor said. He wants to adopt me."

Wren studied his face and went to him. "I want to hear it," she said. "Every word."

"It's still all mixed up in my head. He told me about the

desk and about Peel first, I know that. I didn't say much. I think I said 'So what?' or something."

Wren nodded. "Right. I heard that."

"Anyway. Then he told me he was calling from the hospital, and my heart must have jumped into my throat, then down to my toes. Then he told me it was his stupid ankle bone that zigged when he was zagging. Honest to god, I don't know what I said. Something like, 'I'm glad you're okay,' or whatever. I had this funny lump in my throat. And he knew. He said something I do remember. In fact, I'll never forget it. He said, 'Nicholas, my boy, you mustn't worry about me.' And I said, 'But I do, sir. If it was me, wouldn't you?'" He didn't say anything for a long time, and I said, 'Are you there?' and he said he was. Then he said that it had occurred to him that since we were both alone, with no families or anything, that it might be a happy thought to join forces. He said he wanted to adopt me . . . and was I willing?"

Wren looked up at him and smiled softly. "It's like *As the World Turns,* practically. What did you say? If you said no, I'm going to beat you to death with those Styrofoam potato chips, one chip at a time."

"I told him yes," said Nicholas soberly. "He's a hell of a guy, and I think I love him, even if it sounds funny. I haven't had a father in a long time. The whole idea feels so *strange.*"

"It doesn't sound funny," said Wren.

He stroked her hair softly, his eyes gentle. "I'm a very lucky guy," he said quietly.

"So's your old man," said Wren.

"Mr. Gilliat can see you now," said Mrs. Gosset.

Roland Swain nodded politely and followed the secretary into the inner office. From behind his desk, Harold Gilliat rose in welcome.

A French Finish

"Good morning, Mr. Swain. Sorry to keep you waiting; an urgent call from a rather small lawyer who wants us to sell a rather large estate. It took a bit more time than I'd hoped. But please do sit down, sir."

"Thank you, Mr. Gilliat. It's good of you to see me on such very short notice," said Swain urbanely. "I'm afraid my call must have disarranged your schedule. You do make a visitor to your shores feel most welcome, I must say."

Gilliat smiled. "As a matter of fact, that's how I got to be president, Mr. Swain. I have nine cousins, two brothers and a sister, and a regiment of aunts and uncles. *They* are very difficult to see. The way I work it, I'm here to see you when you call for an appointment. Simple as that. Therefore, sir, what may we do to help you?"

"How I admire the American style," murmured Swain. "In England these preliminaries and overtures may take twenty or thirty minutes of chat. You've done it in something under a minute. Admirable. You go straight to the point, sir. Let me try to do the same. I have some reason to believe that a very valuable Oeben-Riesener *bureau du roi* is currently under discussion. I am here to talk to you about that writing table."

Harold Gilliat shook his head. "The antique world never ceases to amaze me, Mr. Swain. We have not yet concluded our discussions with the owner, and the underground rumors fan out across the world. *Voilà!* Here sits Mr. Roland Swain. I take it you've come to New York from London?"

"So I have, Mr. Gilliat. To correct a slight misunderstanding, I think."

"Misunderstanding?"

"Precisely. You say that you have not yet concluded your discussions with the owner of the Oeben-Riesener. In point of fact, Mr. Gilliat, they have not yet begun. As it happens, sir, I represent a very strong interest in that writing table."

Robert Ross

Harold Gilliat slapped the palm of his hand on his desk. "I *knew* it!" he said triumphantly. "Mr. Otter is an impressive young fellow. But young, Mr. Swain. Very young. There had to be an older, wiser hand on the tiller. I was sure of it!"

"You are most understanding," said Swain.

"Look here," said Gilliat, leaning forward confidentially. "This strong interest you represent—it's Mr. Becker, isn't it? Is he willing to consider our offer? Or has he authorized us to sell the whole package? Otter promised to confer with Mr. Becker; I'm very eager to know what he said, sir."

Swain touched a vein in his temple that, unaccountably, twinged with a sudden pain. "You . . . ah . . . know Mr. Becker?" he said faintly.

Gilliat's eyes narrowed. "I've said too much. I can see that, sir."

"Do . . . you . . . know . . . Becker?" said Swain, measuring out each word with a slow intensity.

My god, thought Gilliat. *Another Anonymity Nut. Tread easy. You'll blow the thing right out of the water unless you handle this one just right.*

"Gilliat's policy is well known," he said amiably. "If Mr. Becker wants to come forward, then we know him. If he prefers to remain in the background, then we do *not* know him. That's our policy, Mr. Swain."

"And as auctioneers, is it also Gilliat's policy that an owner must come forward, sir?" said Swain.

"Absolutely," said Harold Gilliat. "The buyer, whoever he may be, is entitled to a clear title and a notarized receipt signed by all legal owners. That's standard practice, sir."

Roland Swain leaned back and sighed. It was done. "I'm also impressed by your prudence, Mr. Gilliat. You've answered my questions most forthrightly. As for the *bureau du roi,* it's at my hotel. Do you suppose your people might arrange to pick it up and bring it here?"

178

"Of course. And your hotel is . . ."

"The Plaza. I'm so sorry. Room eleven-seventeen."

Gilliat made a hasty note on his desk pad. "That's it, then. I'll have them there in the next hour, if that's convenient, Mr. Swain."

"Thank you, Mr. Gilliat. That will do nicely. I'll go directly back."

"Happy to be of service, Mr. Swain."

"The pleasure," said Swain, "is mine, I assure you."

"Are you sure you want *me* to drop this ball of fuzz on Mr. Gilliat?" said Wren. "I mean, I hardly said a word to the man. He may not even recognize my voice. You did the talking, and I don't see why you—"

"Go ahead and call," said Nicholas. "The professor can't, because he's not supposed to be wired in that tight to us. And Gilliat likes you better than he likes me. You're prettier. So just call and tell him . . . tell him part of the truth. The desk is going to be delivered, but there's been a bit of a delay. I'm out working on it. But *don't* tell him it was hijacked. Keep it simple. Got it?"

"Simple, he says," muttered Wren. She propped the number on the phone and dialed carefully. "What if he starts asking questions? Like—" Gilliat's operator came on the line.

"Mr. Harold Gilliat, please," said Wren.

"One moment, please." There was a short silence. "He's dictating at the moment. May we know who is calling, please?"

Wren gave her name. There was another silence, and suddenly Harold Gilliat's voice came booming over the line.

"Hel-lo, Miss Wooding! How nice to hear from you."

"Mr. Gilliat? You remember me? The desk? Nicholas Otter?"

"Of course I remember you, Miss Wooding. That's how I got to be president. As a matter of fact, I've been expecting your call. What do you think of that?"

Wren twisted her face into a silent shout, summoning Nicholas frantically. She tilted the phone so they both could listen.

"You've been . . . er . . . expecting our call? Uh, heh-heh. Imagine that."

"Very sensible thing to do, Miss Wooding. To call and confirm the delivery to us, I mean."

"Yeah. To confirm the delivery. Right."

"It is, after all, a very valuable piece. And Mr. Swain couldn't have been nicer. He's been and gone, I'm afraid. You couldn't have missed him by more than ten or fifteen minutes. Still, that's pretty good timing, Miss Wooding."

They stared at each other, uncomprehending.

"Mr. . . . uh . . . Swain was there?" said Wren, swallowing hard. "He told you his name?"

"Haven't I said so?" Gilliat's voice was prim. "He's gone back to the Plaza to help our guys load the desk and bring it here. Which reminds me. Will you tell Mr. Otter that we need the papers we talked about—bill of sale, customs clearance, and so on? ASAP?"

"A-sap?"

"As soon as possible, right. Will you tell him?"

"Yeah, sure. You bet, Mr. Gilliat. A-sap."

Wren hung up slowly. "I'd have given maybe eighty-to-one a week ago that we were just about home free. Wow, does the plot ever thicken. What about it, Nicholas? Why does Swain get Peel to steal the goddamn desk from us in Boston, cart it down to New York, and give it to Gilliat's? Doesn't make sense."

"The desk is with Gilliat's. That's good. The professor is okay. That's good. We'll pick him up at the hospital; he's at Phillips House at Massachusetts General. And we'll talk."

180

"You didn't answer my question, Admiral."

"Sure I did. I have to talk to my father."

"It went smoothly, Peel?"

"On its way, sir. Smooth as silk. Gilliat's lorry took it about ten minutes ago."

Roland Swain sighed contentedly. It had been relatively simple to bait the trap after all. Now Becker would have to come out into the open. Owners had to come forward and sign the transfer of title; so Gilliat said, and that was enough. The two young people and the old man were sprats. Becker was the big fish, Swain thought. Gilliat would bring them together, of course.

At the proper moment.

"Might I ask a question, sir?" said Alexander Peel.

"Of course, Peel. What is it?"

"Well, sir, it's like this. I take the desk away from the professor and give it to the Gilliat people. Wouldn't the old man have done the same thing? I'm missing something, but I'm blinked if I know what, sir."

"Mr. Gilliat now accepts me as the representative of Mr. Becker, Peel. When the formal transfer takes place, Mr. Becker must be there, Peel. And so will I."

"Ahhh. So you get to have a bit of a chat with him. The *combine?* Is that it, sir?"

Swain nodded.

"You're deep, Mr. Swain. Too deep for ordinary people, no doubt about it," said Peel.

"Yes, Peel," said Swain, "I know."

Twenty-One

"It's a very ingenious contrivance," said the professor, tapping the cast on his leg proudly. "I can put nearly all of my weight on this lump of plaster they've built up under my heel."

"You hang on to my arm," said Wren grimly, "or you'll fall on your ass again. You've got a soft heart and very brittle bones."

"Yes, my dear," said Tewksbury meekly, "so I've discovered." They inched cautiously up the stairs to the front door, while Nicholas fumbled with the keyhole for a moment, then pushed the door open.

"You want to go upstairs and climb into bed?" asked Nicholas.

"I just got out of bed, damnit," said the old man tartly. "Let's sit around the kitchen table. I'd like a cup of tea, and we've lots of things to talk about."

They trooped slowly down the hall and into the kitchen, where the professor lowered himself carefully into a chair. Wren busied herself with cups and saucers and put a pot of water on to boil.

"First things first," said Tewksbury. "I'm very pleased that you like my idea about the adoption, Nicholas; very pleased. I've thought about it since our brief conversation on the phone, you know."

"So have I," said Nicholas. "It's been stewing in my head all night. All I can say, sir, is that I feel damn good about it."

"That's the important thing, of course. I have the same feeling. It rings with a sense of rightness, if you see what I mean."

"For some reason, I always thought of you as a widower," said Wren. "You know, with four sons living in Vancouver or something. You don't strike me as a bachelor-type person."

Tewksbury smiled at her. "I fell in and out of love frequently when I was a younger man. But when I was young enough to think about marriage, I was too busy with my studies to do anything about it. Mothers steered their eligible daughters around me in a very wide circle; indeed they did. Then, little by little I fell in love with my work. Somehow the years slipped away, and the women who fluttered their eyelashes at me had too much gray in their hair. By then it was too late."

"It sounds like a lonely life," said Nicholas.

"It is, and it isn't, my boy. My colleagues at Harvard helped me to build a good life. And there was always my work. I poured my creative energies into it, I can tell you. It's always been too quiet around the house, I'll admit that. But then, I've had some marvelous housekeepers down through the years. Mrs. Beattie, for example. A *wonderful* woman. I came very near to a proposal with Bridget Beattie, Nicholas. But somehow my work always intervened. She moved to Tampa last year. As for my old friends and colleagues at the university, they are all gone now. I've outlived them all." He sighed.

"Well," said Nicholas, "there will be some new noises around here now. I only hope you won't be sorry."

"Sorry? Not a chance. It's one of the things I look forward to most of all, Nicholas."

"There is this one thing that may be a—"

"It's not a problem at all," interrupted the old man firmly. "I hope that Wren will consent to share our roof. To ask either of you to divide your allegiance would be unthinkable. I'll not have it . . . and we'll say no more about it!"

Wren turned from the stove and went to the professor to kiss him softly on the cheek. "You're a hell of a guy," she said, "and I accept. Also, I love you, even if you are a crook."

Tewksbury shifted with embarrassment, his face pink with pleasure. "There are practical matters to discuss, you know. My estate, for one thing. It's quite substantial. I'll want to revise my will, Nicholas, and name you as my—"

"I don't want to fog this thing up with money," said Nicholas. "We're going to be just fine, and I hope you'll leave your will just the way it is. I don't need the money, sir. I need a father. Let's not confuse things, okay?"

"And then there's this house," said the professor. "When I'm gone, must it be sold? I confess that the idea distresses me. Won't you take it, my boy? Please."

Nicholas hesitated, and Wren came over and tapped him on the top of his head with a teaspoon. "Say yes, dumbhead. Don't sit there and think. You always think too goddamn much. Just say yes."

"Yes," said Nicholas. "Thank you, sir."

The old man nodded happily.

"There's one thing, sir. My name. Do I need to change my name? How does that work, do you know?"

"It's not the perpetuation of the name I'm after, Nicholas. It's the chance to share some of the pleasures and the pains of life together. That's what I care about. Your parents gave you a name. Why not keep it?"

"You know that Nicholas and I live in sin," said Wren. "Or whatever they called it in 1910. Are you uptight about that? I mean, should we tiptoe over to the Sonesta Motel on the Charles River and register as Mr. and Mrs. Bonwit Teller?"

"You live here," said the professor. "Why make it complicated?"

"Wow," said Wren. "What a father. Maybe you could adopt me, too."

"I'm rather attracted to the notion of standing at your side to give you away at the altar," said Tewksbury. "As for adopting you, don't be greedy. You *have* a father."

"Right," said Nicholas. "Don't be greedy. And we're not ready for the big M." He peered at Wren. "Are we?"

"I'd say you need browning on the other side, and a few more hours in the oven," said Wren thoughtfully. "When you're really cooked, you'll be the first to know."

"Did I tell you that I own a motorcar?" said Tewksbury suddenly. "It's in the garage behind the yard. I haven't driven it in more years than I care to think about. But I'm sure it runs; I have it looked at once a year, like clockwork."

"Once a *year?*" said Wren.

"Yes indeed. For the Antique Car Parade. It purrs along very sweetly. I don't drive it myself, as I say. I ride in the back, dressed like a passenger."

"Uh . . . what kind of a car is it?" said Wren.

"A Hupmobile," said Tewksbury. "Nineteen-twenty-seven."

"Hupmobile? Who would give a car a name like that?"

"Mr. Hupp, of course," said the professor stiffly. "A damn fine piece of engineering, too."

"But . . . but don't the tires go *flat?*" said Wren. "My god. They're fifty years old!"

"The tires are solid rubber, and the tread is still good and deep. It's a *good* car, and I'm giving it to my new son—and that's a decision!" Tewksbury smiled. "I never thought I'd be able to give my son a car. What a nice feeling."

"Listen," said Nicholas, "I think I'm almost afraid to drive the thing. But by god, if my father wants to give me a car, I'm going to take it. I like the idea a whole hell of a lot. Can I have the keys to the car, Dad?"

"Sure can, son," said Tewksbury, laughing.

"You guys are *nuts*," said Wren. "But what the hell. What color is the upholstery? I might as well play, too."

"Gray," said Tewksbury. "Gray corduroy."

"Wow," said Wren.

"I was going to have a long talk about Roland Swain," said Nicholas, "but this has been a hell of a lot better."

Tewksbury nodded. "He's not going to tell us what he has up his sleeve, so why worry? Gilliat's have our desk, so we will all go down to New York for the Evening Sale next month. Meanwhile, I suggest that we start to find out what it's like to live together. I'm going to call a lawyer I know and start the adoption proceedings and change the title and deed to the house and . . . and a few other things. Meanwhile, Nicholas can learn to drive the car. And Wren can concentrate on cooking Nicholas until he's browned on both sides."

"Now, *that's* what I call fatherly advice," said Wren. "Here's your tea. Pour."

Twenty-Two

Half-past seven.

Thirty minutes more.

Nicholas fingered the golden Becker in his pocket. He surveyed the crowded Sale Room.

"I'm a little nervous," he whispered to Wren.

"*You're* nervous?" muttered Wren. "I'm so tight that if you say one wrong word to me, I'll bite you in the neck. Don't talk to me about nervous. What are you doing in your pocket? I can see your fingers wiggling."

"I'm rubbing my Becker."

"You watch your goddamn mouth. I'm in no mood to—"

"Becker, Wren, Becker. My lucky coin."

"Oh-ho. Becker. Where do we sit? Do you see the professor? Is Swain here? You got a catalog? What lot number are we? How much do you think we'll sell—?"

"Turn off the faucet," he said softly. "Here comes Gilliat."

Down the center aisle that divided the Sale Room, Harold Gilliat swept toward them, impenetrable dignity in every step. He wore a dark blue suit with a vest that displayed a thin golden chain stretched from pocket to pocket. His shirt was white, his tie a solid dark blue. He shook hands with them formally, taking a cautious look to each side.

"How do you like my costume?" he whispered.

"Who's dead?" said Wren. "Four of your cousins?"

Gilliat smiled. "This is my major-money outfit, Miss Wooding. I drag it out and wear it whenever I think we've got a chance to get a million or more from one item. It's my lucky suit."

"Yeah. Nicholas has this lucky—" She winced as Nicholas planted a shoe squarely on her foot. "I think you broke my big toe."

"It's my business," said Nicholas quietly.

"Your business," said Wren. "Yeah, I see what you mean."

"I wanted to thank you for sending all the documents down from Boston," said Gilliat. "They were in perfect order . . . and that doesn't happen all the time, I can tell you. It did surprise me a bit, though. You and Miss Wooding here are recorded and confirmed as the only owners of the desk, the letter, and the jewels." He lowered his voice to the faintest of whispers. "What about . . . you-know-who?"

"You mean Mr. Becker?" whispered Nicholas.

Gilliat nodded.

"He told us he flipped a coin and decided to stay out of sight. He likes to remain—"

"I know. Anonymous," murmured Gilliat. "I understand. You're authorized to sign for him. Happens all the time. Look, Nick. Did you talk to him about packaging the whole thing for one sale? You sent the documents for the desk and the letter and the jewels, so I thought maybe the package thing was still open."

Nicholas shook his head. "Just the desk, Mr. Gilliat."

"But did you see the New York papers? We made the front page of the New York *Times,* believe it or not. First time since 1922, when some railroad tycoon bought the Braganza diamond from us for half a million. I've had every major dealer in the country chewing on me for tickets to this sale. There must be at least ten secret bidders here tonight from the major collectors . . . and another ten I've never seen before. Follow me? No tourists tonight, Nick. This is a crowd of buyers."

"But you'll still buy us out for six," said Nicholas. "Right?"

"Sure. That still goes. I've worn this suit before . . . and bombed out. You just never know. Your desk can still get hung up at five hundred and five thousand for no damn reason in the world. That happens all the time, too."

"No doubt," said Nicholas. "But for the moment, just the desk."

Gilliat dipped his head fractionally. "You're probably right." He swung his gaze to the doorway. "Hoo boy. Here's the Mellon Museum and the Met. I've got to leave you . . . and, good luck." He made a small bow and moved slowly off.

"I don't see the professor," said Wren.

"Up front. First row. There's a big fat guy with a bald head on his right. See him?"

Wren nodded. "Why did he sit where we can't see each other?"

"More room to stretch his leg. The cast is uncomfortable. That's what he said, anyway. My guess is that he didn't want us looking back and forth at each other. This crowd has a very fast set of eyeballs, Redbird. We're not supposed to be friends, remember? That's the party line."

"Shouldn't we sit?" said Wren. "This place is filling up fast. Same place, over near the side?"

Nicholas handed her his briefcase and pulled the golden coin from his pocket and flipped it deftly. "Heads," he announced. "Right. Same seats, same row as before."

In his small office just offstage, Piers Shaw-Alcott studied the white card carefully. Following Gilliat's established practice, he had listed the names of the major bidders who had requested that he recognize a secret bidding signal. He glanced calmly at his watch. Twenty minutes. More than enough time to memorize them all.

There were five blinkers, he noted wryly. Peckham, from the Cleveland Museum, would blink once to signal his bid. Also Asprey. Dunlea. And the two dealers from Chicago. He marked a tiny B beside each of the five names.

Next, John Kimball and his pipe. In the mouth—to bid. Out of the mouth—to pass. He added a P to his list.

Three finger-lifters, including two women he had never seen before. One pencil-tapper would touch the pencil to his lips. Another woman he had never seen before—she would touch her locket to signal her bid, or leave it alone to pass. A tiny L went beside her name.

He completed the list, then reviewed it several times. It was essential, he knew, to see each secret signal—but not to be seen doing so. Kimball, for example, specifically requested that the head auctioneer pick up his bid and then turn away and look to the other side of the room—and call it only then. It was a tricky bit of business, but when it all went smoothly, it never failed to spur the bidding forward.

Satisfied at last, Shaw-Alcott put the card into his folder

and turned his attention to the list of reserve prices. How much time? He glanced at his watch again. Seven minutes to go now.

From behind the partly open door to the Sale Room, Roland Swain watched Nicholas and Wren settle into their seats. When he saw that they were safely occupied with the sale catalog, he drifted unobtrusively into the room and down the center aisle to the row directly behind them. Then he too opened his catalog, bending over its pages.

There would be one hundred and fifty-two lots offered for sale tonight, he noted. The *bureau du roi,* a late entry, had been photographed in color and a copy print inserted at the front, stapled to a brief descriptive statement. It had been numbered as Lot 122-A. Swain checked his watch. Five minutes to eight. Cautiously he studied the faces around him . Could one of them be Becker? Probably not, he thought. Becker would be too wily to risk it. Tomorrow, then; Gilliat's office—where payment must be completed, documents exchanged, and arrangements for delivery made. It had to be so; common sense compelled it.

"How did I end up holding your goddamn briefcase in *my* lap?" said Wren. "It's heavy. What are you carrying in here?" She shifted the case awkwardly. Nicholas reached over and took it from her.

"I thought you might want to lean your sale catalog on it. I'll take it. And hang on tight; here comes Shaw-Alcott."

Gilliat's head auctioneer walked slowly across the low platform stage at the front of the room, a manila folder under one arm. His manner, as always, was stately, and even his dignified nod to one or two familiar faces had something regal about it. From behind the lectern he lifted the ivory cube and watched the second hand of the clock on the wall sweep toward twelve. Eight o'clock. The cube clicked against the block of ebony, making a clear sound in the silent room.

"Good evening, ladies and gentlemen. Tonight we present one hundred and fifty-two lots, comprising an assortment of English, French, and Colonial furniture, bronzes, works of art—including the Codrington miniatures, and four enamel-and-hardstone ornamental objects by Fabergé. We also call your attention to Lot 122-A, which has been inserted in the front of your catalog. Standard terms and conditions shall apply. These may be found in the back of the catalog. I am now required by law to remind you all that bidders must assume that a reserve price has been set on all lots. May I have Lot One, please?"

Shaw-Alcott turned to watch an aide bring forward a small wooden chest, boldly carved with scenes of the hunt. While the chest was being shown, the auctioneer studied the crowd. It feels like a cautious group, he thought, his face impassive.

Too quiet, thought Harold Gilliat. They're too damn quiet. He stood in his accustomed place at the very back of the room, directly under the big clock on the wall. The bidding for Lot One was desultory; no lift, no life to it; no sense of competition. We're going to bomb, he thought. Shaw-Alcott will work for every dime tonight. He sucked moodily on a tooth and listened.

"And seven hundred I have, seven I have . . . may I hear eight? Eight. Eight. Seven-*fifty* I have, and thank you, madam. Seven-fifty I have, may I *now* hear eight? Thank you, sir. I have eight. Nine. Nine. Nine. Do I have nine? A very fine piece, ladies and gentlemen—original wood and hardware—a twelfth-century personal chest that may—I

now have nine from the gentleman in the third row. May I
now hear one thousand?"

Slowly Shaw-Alcott teased the price upward. He was
sharply aware that these first few lots must not be knocked
down at depressed prices. It would alert the bidders to a fa-
tal vulnerability, and the bidding would be low all night.
The carved wooden chest caught one collector at nine
hundred and ninety-five dollars, where the bidding simply
dried up.

"And done," intoned Shaw-Alcott. "Sold to the Cowper
Gallery. May we have Lot Two, please?"

"It sounds sort of dull," said Wren about an hour later.
"We're up to Lot Seventy-four, and the whole thing feels
like a big nothing. Is it my imagination, or is everyone waiting for our writing table?"

Nicholas shook his head. "Hard to say. The Codrington
miniatures are coming up soon. Let's see how they go."

The tall, balding man on Tewksbury's right nudged him
gently with an elbow. "Excuse me," he whispered hoarsely,
"but this is my first big auction. If I want to bid, what do I
do? I mean, do I just raise my hand like we do up in Tarry-
town? I don't see people making bids, but he's calling 'em
out. See what I mean?"

Tewksbury turned and studied the man, who seemed
genuinely embarrassed. "I'm Jim Freshwater," the bald
man added. "Should have introduced myself. I'm here for
my wife."

"How do you do, Mr. Freshwater," Tewksbury murmured. "There's quite a lot of code bidding going on here
tonight; more than you generally find. You don't see it because you're not supposed to see it, if you follow me."
Freshwater nodded.

"Then what do I do? Raise my hand, like I said?"

"If you wish. Shaw-Alcott is one of the best; indeed, a single finger will do very nicely." Tewksbury waggled his own finger, by way of demonstration.

"*Thank* you, Professor Tewksbury," said Shaw-Alcott, the faintest note of surprise in his voice. "We now have fourteen thousand, five hundred bid by the well-known expert, Professor Lewis Poe Tewksbury, for this champlevé enamel-and-bronze jardiniere, flanked by those two delightful gilt-bronze cherubs on the shaped white-onyx base. Fourteen-five I have, may I hear fifteen. If the learned—I *do* have fifteen; thank you, madam. May I now hear sixteen? Sixteen?"

"Jee-zuzz," said Wren, "what does he want with that monstrosity? It looks like something the Elks used to use for a second prize on Bingo Night."

"Quiet," said Nicholas. "The Codrington miniatures are next. This place needs something to get it going. Maybe this is it."

"I bet you that's why the professor bid on that big pot," said Wren suddenly. "To get things going, I mean."

"Lot One Hundred," said Shaw-Alcott. "The magnificent carved-ivory set of the twelve apostles, dated and authenticated by Reiter, Ellman, and Dr. Burrell-Lovitz for the period from *anno Domini* 950 to 1050. Of walrus tusk, produced by an unknown artisan, probably of an early Cistercian monastic order. The portraiture and handling of the draped garments is exceptionally fine, and the set is complete. Reference to this work may be found in church literature, and it was held by eleven generations of the Codrington family before it came on the market about a century ago. The set is unique, ladies and gentlemen."

An attendant held up the red morocco tray so that all might see. A thousand years of aging had imparted a soft, dark-honey shade to the twelve tiny statues; each piece seemed to glow with life. How lovingly it had been wrought, what a marvel of reverence, Tewksbury thought. There is more truth in these little figures than in any treaty.

"One hundred and sixty-two thousand I have," said Shaw-Alcott. One-six-two; may I hear one-six-five? One-six-five. One-six-three, I have, from Mr. Bucharest; thank you, sir. One-six-three; one hundred and sixty-three thousand dollars?" The auctioneer paused only a fraction of a second more. "And *done*. Sold to Mr. Martin Bucharest."

"Listen," said Nicholas tensely, "I've got some bad news."

"If you've missed two periods in a row, I'll do the right thing," said Wren.

"I'm serious, for Christ's sake. The miniatures just went for one-sixty-three. They had an estimated bidding range of one-fifty to four hundred thousand. This is a dead crowd, and unless we do something, we're going to sell that desk for peanuts."

"What do you call peanuts?"

"Goddamn if I know. One of those Fabergé things had a top of forty thousand. Shaw-Alcott worked like a horse and barely got fourteen. The Codringtons were one-six-three, like I say. It's been like that all night."

"So we only get two hundred thousand dollars, okay? What's the matter with two hundred thousand dollars? I happen to have a great deal of respect and admiration for two hundred thousand dollars. So why not take it and run?"

"Absolutely not," said Nicholas. "We had expenses, remember? Gilliat's get ten percent, remember? *And* we split three ways. C'mon, Wren. I think we'd better add the letter and the jewels to the deal, just as Gilliat said. What d'you say?"

"Speaking of Gilliat, didn't he offer six hundred thousand dollars? He said that, remember?"

"But not *now*, for Christ's sake! He sees what's happening here, same as we do. If I know him, he'll turn me down and tell me politely that he got to be president that way." Nicholas tightened his lips. "All I know is that we've got to do something. The jewels and the letter are all we've got. You have a vote, so *vote.*"

"Don't put this on me," hissed Wren fiercely. "You're the Admiral. So do something admirable; like, use your head!"

Nicholas stared at her, a smile forming. "Use my head. Of course!" He fumbled in his pocket and extracted the gold coin triumphantly. "Use my head and my tail, Redbird! I should have thought of this right away. Ready? I'll flip it, and you catch it, okay? We're partners . . . so here *goes.*"

The coin shot up, end over end, and as Wren reached over to trap it on its downward flight—she missed. It struck the side of her hand and fell to the floor with an audible clink, spun twice, and rolled to rest directly between the toes of Roland Swain's polished boots. Reaching down, he picked it up to examine it, and the first twisting pang of suspicion flared in his mind.

Wren turned around, her hand outstretched. "Did you see where it went?" she said. "I dropped our Becker." Recognition struck her dumb, and she could only pull weakly at Nicholas' shoulder.

"It's not down there, Admiral," she said. "Straighten up and see the nice man who found your nifty lucky piece."

"May we have Lot One-fifteen?" said Shaw-Alcott.

Twenty-Three

"Now, look, Mr. Swain," said Harold Gilliat grimly, "I cannot stand out here in the hall and have a little chat. You and Mr. Otter will have to see me in the morning. I've got a disaster on my hands in there, and the *bureau du roi* is the only hope I've got left. Now, if you will excuse me—"

"The disaster, sir, is right here in my hand," said Roland Swain tightly. "That's what I'm trying to get you to understand." He held up the golden coin, as though it explained everything. Peel stood behind him.

"So?" said Gilliat.

"That sir, is Becker," said Swain.

"Yes, I see that. It's a Becker."

"Not *a* Becker, Mr. Gilliat. *The* Becker. Don't you understand? This is Mr. Otter's so-called secret partner. This is Carl Becker—except there is no Carl Becker, of course!"

Swain cast a venomous look at Nicholas. "He knows what I'm talking about."

"Well, I do not," said Gilliat. "We'll have to sort it all out in the morning. Or tonight, after the sale. Right now, I must get back in there and—"

"Hold it," said Nicholas. "I want to add the letter and the jewels to the deal and get bids on all three. Is it too late to do that?"

Gilliat bit at his lip. "Yes," he said thoughtfully, "that might do it. Can do. But I'll have to hurry." He darted through the door and back into the room, striding swiftly down the aisle toward Shaw-Alcott, oblivious to the heads that craned to stare. Swain watched him, his fingers working desperately. "The desk is a fake, the letter is a fake, Becker is a fake," he snapped, pitching the golden coin at Nicholas. "And you, Mr. Otter, are a fake, as well! I'm going in there and stop that sale and expose the lot of you!"

Nicholas opened his briefcase and fished out a portable tape recorder. "Do yourself a favor, Mr. Swain. Take this into the men's room or something . . . and listen to it. You can keep it, in fact. We made lots of duplicates—all ready to mail out. You planted some microphones on us, so we did it to you, too. I'm not saying you can't go back in there and blow us out of the water. I'm only saying you really ought to listen to this stuff first. Peel calls you by name, you call him by name, and tape recordings are admissible as evidence these days, Mr. Swain. You follow?" Nicholas punched the button of the little recorder. "You'll remember this one, I think," he murmured. The reels rotated slowly for a moment; then Swain's voice could be heard: *"To say it plainly, young man, you and your friends have invaded my territory. Others have tried it, of course. I say to you now what I have said to them. My associates and I control the fake-antique market. We function somewhat* beyond the limits of the law, so the conventional recourse to the police and to the courts is not available to us. In consequence, we have learned to administer our own law—and the punishment for its transgression."

The taped sound of the voice of Nicholas seemed unimpressed: *"That's a lot of words."*

Now Swain's tone took on a deadly edge: *"True, but hardly idle ones. Your young lady might be found in one of the canals here, quite dead. Mr. Peel has my orders to smother her quickly and drop her in. He will do so. You must understand that. He has done so for me many, many times."*

Swain stared at the recorder, his face a mask of fury. Nicholas depressed a button, and the recorder stopped.

"I want you to understand something, Mr. Swain. And you, too, Mr. Peel. If anything happens to the professor or to Wren Wooding or to Caspar Planchet or to me—and I mean *anything*—copies of this tape go to Scotland Yard, every major London paper, *and* the BBC. You two ought to pray that we stay healthy for a long, long time. Because if we don't you two are going to be very famous jailbirds. Do I make myself clear? Nicholas pushed an unresisting Peel away from the door with a gentle nudge of a finger and walked back into the Sale Room.

"What do we do *now*, sir?" said Alexander Peel.

"Do? We leave quietly, Mr. Peel. We pack our bags and get on a plane that will take us home. I've underestimated that young man. We lose, Mr. Peel, we lose." A philosophic note touched Swain's voice. "Round one, at least."

"I have just been handed a message from the president of our company," said Shaw-Alcott. "It states that he wishes to make a brief announcement at this time. Ladies and gentlemen, Mr. Harold Gilliat."

"Thank you, Piers," said Gilliat easily. "This is an almost

unprecedented occurrence, ladies and gentlemen. It has happened just once before in our company's long history— when certain unusual circumstances caused my grandfather to rise to interrupt the proceedings. The circumstances then, while interesting, are not germane. The circumstances tonight, as I think you will shortly agree, are most germane." He paused, as though to gather his thoughts, then continued.

"I will be brief. The owners of Lot 122-A, the Oeben-Riesener *bureau du roi,* have—just moments ago—agreed to our recommendation to include the now-famous letter from Marie Antoinette in the sale tonight. They have also agreed to include the elegant little collection of diamonds, rubies, emeralds, and pearls found in the secret compartments of this same desk."

He paused, and a small pocket of silence was at once filled by a long buzzing sound that rolled across the room. Gilliat lifted his hand, commanding attention once again.

"Gilliat's takes full responsibility for this interruption, and, indeed, we are proud to do so. Ladies and gentlemen, these beautiful objects have shared a strange destiny— together. We believe they should be allowed to remain together. Therefore, I now ask Mr. Shaw-Alcott to resume the proceedings of the Evening Sale and to accept your bids for Lot 122-A, which now comprises the desk, the jewels, and the letter. I thank you."

A furor of voices erupted at once. At the side of the room, John Kimball sprang to his feet, thrusting his pipe aloft and demanding to be heard.

"I'm authorized to bid on the desk—and only on the desk!" he shouted.

"Right!" called another voice. "I'm in the same boat!"

"You can't do this!" screamed a frantic young man. "It's *illegal!*"

A French Finish

Professor Tewksbury rose slowly and turned to face the sea of angry and confused faces. Like a rueful teacher who expects his brilliant class of students to behave, he held up a single admonishing finger. Magically, the hubbub subsided at once.

"Please forgive my intrusion, Mr. Gilliat . . . and ladies and gentlemen. But perhaps I can be of some small assistance. What is happening here tonight has happened before. I've been attending these wonderful events for fifty years, you see. I recall similar situations in Paris, in Geneva, in Rome, and in London. And here in New York, as Mr. Gilliat has already said. In the cases I refer to, a brief recess was declared. All who then wished to do so could consult with their principals for fresh instructions. Here in this very building, I venture to say that there are enough private offices—and private telephones—to serve all who need them. Why not declare a thirty-minute recess, Mr. Gilliat? There are many many fine people who have been placed in a most difficult position. Perhaps my suggestion might relieve that difficulty, sir. If you approve—and if those here tonight approve—of course."

Diffidently the old man raised his cane in half-salute and limped carefully back to his seat. The crowd broke into long applause, and one exuberant whistle sounded piercingly from the back of the room.

His dark face alight, Harold Gilliat tapped on the lectern with his knuckle.

"I do declare a thirty-minute recess, as proposed so wisely by Professor Tewksbury. All those who wish to make use of one of our private offices will please meet me in the reception area on the floor above. Those of you who have graciously consented to wait will be served a complimentary cup of coffee from our coffee machine. It is, I say with some pride, the vilest brew to be had on Manhattan Island!" He grinned boyishly.

There was some more applause and good-natured laughter. Here and there a few people rose and stretched.

"What happened to Swain?" muttered Wren. "No. I take it back. Don't tell me. Another thing. Where are the jewels and the letter? Peel took the desk, right? But where is the other stuff—in Boston? I'll bet it's in Boston. What an operation."

"The professor and I decided to put the letter and the jewels back in the desk," said Nicholas placidly. "Far as I know, they're still there. Swain didn't know where the secret compartments were. Neither did Peel. So that's where they are."

"Famous last words," said Wren. "I'm going to double-check. You want to come?"

"No, you go ahead. I want to think."

The *bureau du roi,* now standing well forward on the platform, was surrounded by a small circle of people. Wren knelt at the center drawer, carefully pressing and rotating the golden ornament that decorated the keyhole. A narrow edge next to the drawer slid forward fractionally, allowing her fingers just enough purchase to pull it out fully. It was an astonishing little drawer, no more than six inches wide and an eighth of an inch deep. Gently, Wren lifted the letter out and placed it on the desk's surface. She pressed the drawer back into its seat, rotated the ornament back to its original position, and moved to the left-front leg of the desk. Feeling beneath the top, she found the head of the false wood screw and pressed firmly. The crowd of onlookers gasped. The whole front of the table's leg swung open. Wren plucked the chamois bag full of gems from its receptacle and clicked the panel shut.

Retrieving the letter, she brought them to Shaw-Alcott, who stood at his lectern a few steps away.

"You'll need these," said Wren. "I'm one of the owners."

A French Finish

"How do you do, Miss Wooding," said Shaw-Alcott. "We'll take very good care of these, of course."

"You know me?" said Wren, surprised.

"Indeed. We disposed of your clocks and coins not too many months ago, did we not? It may interest you to know that your grandfather acquired them in this very room. A fine gentleman, Miss Wooding. It was an honor to know him. Yes, your grandfather was one of our most loyal customers."

"Wow," said Wren. "I wish he could see me now. I think."

Twenty-Four

"How about a cup of coffee, professor?" said Mr. Freshwater. "You've got a bum leg, and I'd be more happy to bring it to you; just say the word."

"Thank you . . . but no," said Tewksbury. "I've sampled Gilliat's coffee in times past. It *is* undrinkable, in my opinion. But you go right ahead, sir. I'll watch your seat, never fear." Freshwater nodded his appreciation and ambled off.

Tewksbury turned to look around. People clustered everywhere, chatting amiably; rivals unbent to talk shop and exchange improbable rumors. Somehow, the unexpected recess had lightened the atmosphere; a sense of anticipation and good cheer permeated the room.

Harold Gilliat sat down beside the old man. Gone was the frown; a broad smile lit his features. "Eleven of them wanted to call their principals, and we have exactly eleven private offices. It's working like a Swiss watch. Mind if we visit a bit?"

"Not at all, Mr. Gilliat. Mr. Freshwater has gone off for some of your coffee; let us pray that he returns."

Gilliat laughed. "I had to stop to say that we owe you a yard and a half of thanks, professor. Brilliant suggestion, sir, just brilliant." Gilliat's voice lowered conspiratorially. "You've saved this sale tonight, and that's the truth."

"You're much too generous," said Tewksbury. "I'm sure the same thought crossed your mind. Didn't your grandfather adopt that very tactic many years ago?"

"True, true. But it came from you, professor, and that's what made the difference. People in this business know you, sir. They respect your integrity, and when you have something to say, they listen. I hope you know that. Most of the killer sharks in our business are here tonight; there are damn few human beings they'll trust, believe me. But they respect you. If the recess had been my idea, we'd still be arguing. Instead, they're sitting here like lambs, ready to bid."

"It's kind of you to say so, Mr. Gilliat; very kind."

"Take this lovely little desk," said Gilliat. The *bureau du roi* had been brought to the very front of the platform, standing just to the right of the lectern. "It's a perfect case in point. Did we have solid authentication? We did not. We had some opinions from Dr. Duclos and François Varenne; but *opinions*, sir. On a television show, no less! That's what my people in Paris told me."

"Quite true, too," said Tewksbury. "I was on the same program, as you must have been told."

"That's the point, that's the point. You were skeptical, isn't that right? I was told that you challenged the authenticity of the desk."

"And so I did."

"And yet, here you are," murmured Gilliat. "The killer sharks know about Paris, too, professor. They know you were dubious . . . and now they see you here. Obviously, you've changed our mind. So they are prepared to bid. It's your reputation that does it, sir."

"Changed my mind? Whoever told you that I had changed my mind, Mr. Gilliat?" Tewksbury shook his head primly. "I haven't changed my mind at all," he said.

Gilliat stiffened in his seat and turned to stare at the old man, genuinely shocked. "Are you telling me that you think that desk sitting up there is a fake?" he whispered.

"It may well be, Mr. Gilliat. I have great respect for Duclos and Varenne, but the plain fact is that no tests have been made. Until they are, how can I be sure? Indeed, how can—?"

"My god," said Gilliat, "but you gave me a fright." He looked around for eavesdroppers. "I'm going to tell you something I'd rather you didn't noise around, and I'm telling you because I trust you. The net-net is sensational. I did run tests—a full battery of them—on that table. Opinions on television are nice, professor. But in my business they're like a promise written on water, you know? I had to make sure."

"Your secret is safe," said Tewksbury. "It was prudent of you, I must say. Am I permitted to ask what the tests revealed?"

"The desk is here, isn't it?" said Gilliat complacently. "If that thing is a fake, it fooled every test in the book!"

"I'm impressed," said the professor, "more than you can know."

"And I went beyond the technology. Believe me I did. I've had some very painful lessons in this job, and I've learned where to look. I can spot the fake aging by a veneering hammer or a molding scratcher or a chipper in nothing flat. That surface is genuine, professor. I'll stake my job on it!" He grimaced. "My god, what am I saying?"

"I didn't hear a word," said the professor solemnly.

"And then, I spent a lot of time examining the drawer in that desk," said Gilliat. "These old masters had their own way of joining the wood at the corners. Some of them followed the fashions in dovetailing, and you can often date their work that way. Others ignored the fashions, and if they liked the covered dovetail, they stayed with it. Oeben liked the straight mitered dovetail. Riesener preferred the slot dovetail. That desk may carry both names, but it's Riesener's. No doubt about it. Then, there's the glue; the modern faker won't take the trouble to render the hoof of a horse to make his glue. But I put a bit of the glue on that desk through the lab. Horse's hoof, professor."

"Any drawer guides?" said Tewksbury. "I never did think to look."

"Certainly not. I wish I had a dollar for every drawer guide I've found on furniture that's supposed to be two or three hundred years old. And, naturally, I looked for signs of a power saw—it's a dead giveaway. Those old marquetry saws were worked by a foot treadle, of course. It makes for a subtle variation in the cuts, and that's what I found on our little desk! I could go on and on, but you can see what I'm driving at. That *bureau du roi* passed every test I could think of—with flying colors."

Professor Tewksbury frowned slightly. "What puzzles me, Mr. Gilliat, is your zeal. Auction houses make it a firm policy to do no authentication on their own. That's your policy, too, isn't it? Then . . . why these costly tests?"

Harold Gilliat shook his finger. "Oh, no. You'll have to let me have a few secrets of my own, professor. But I'll give you a hint. You watch the bidding, okay? No offense, sir. It's just that we want to keep it secret for a bit."

"I understand completely," said Tewksbury mildly. "We all have our little secrets."

Gilliat rose as Mr. Freshwater approached, a plastic coffee cup in his hand.

"You're actually drinking that stuff?" said Tewksbury.

"Hell," said the bald man, "it's not great coffee, but it's better than Myra makes, for sure."

"Thank you for letting me use your seat," said Gilliat. "I see Shaw-Alcott. It's about time to put the show on the road." He bowed and left them.

"Very polite fella," said Freshwater. "I can see how he got to be president."

"Thank you for your patience, ladies and gentlemen. I declare the Evening Sale open once again." Shaw-Alcott opened his folder. "We will now take your bids for Lot 122-A—an elegant *bureau du roi* attributed to Oeben and Riesener, with characteristic marquetry, fittings of cast gold, and two secret compartments in which were found a rare letter from Marie Antoinette and a small pouch of pearls and precious stones."

He paused, and an expectant hush fell over the room.

"We will open the bidding for the complete lot . . . at one million dollars, if you please."

A storm of spontaneous applause followed his words, from those who would not bid. But here and there, in isolated pockets of rage, men and women rose, red-faced and demanding to be heard. Shaw-Alcott stood, like the last Spartan at the pass, and faced them down. He stared indifferently at each protester, as though aware that sooner or later sweet reason would prevail. And like reluctant waves that are pulled back by the falling tide, little by little, the clamor subsided.

"May I hear one million?" said the auctioneer.

"Seven hundred and fifty," called a sneering voice.

"Eight," said a voice from the very rear.

"Nine hundred thousand dollars," said a jeweled society matron in the third row.

"The Cleveland Museum bids one million dollars," said Peckham.

"One million I have," said Shaw-Alcott calmly. "May I have one-million-one?"

To the left Kimball puffed gently on his pipe. The auctioneer's eyes swept past him to scan the opposite side of the room carefully.

"One-million-one I have. May I hear one-million-two?"

Near Kimball, a woman blinked, followed a fraction of a second later by yet another bid signaled by a lifted finger.

"I have one-million-two from the right side of the room, about halfway back," said Shaw-Alcott firmly. The finger dropped swiftly. "One-million-two I have, may I have one-million-three? One-three? One-three? If there are no further bids, ladies and—"

Near the front, along the wall, an elderly woman with snow-white hair gazed at the ceiling and let her fingers stray to the heart-shaped golden locket that hung from her neck.

"One-million-three I now have," said Shaw-Alcott. "Do I have four? Four? Do I have four?"

Kimball tapped his pipe softly against his lips.

The auctioneer looked past him to the rear of the room, and then: "One million, three hundred and fifty thousand dollars I am bid." Kimball's pipe puffed its approval. "One-three-five-oh," said Shaw-Alcott. "Do I now have four?"

Again the little locket was barely touched.

"I have one million, three hundred and sixty thousand," said the auctioneer. One million, three-sixty? Are there no more—?"

Kimball's pipe now tapped very slowly against his lower teeth.

"I have one million, three-sixty-five."

Now a single finger touched the little golden locket.

". . . and sixty-six I have."

Kimball's pipe tapped at a tooth once more.

". . . and sixty-*seven*."

The locket stirred.

". . . and eight."

The pipe tapped.

"*And* nine. I now have one million, three hundred and sixty-nine thousand dollars bid; one million, three-six-nine. Do I have—?" Again the locket stirred. "I *do* have one million, three hundred and seventy thousand dollars, thank you very much."

Shaw-Alcott, his gaze turned well away from Kimball, watched the pipe from the edge of his eye. It rose slowly . . . to be slipped into a pocket, and it was seen no more. "I have one million, three hundred and seventy thousand dollars bid on Lot 122-A, ladies and gentlemen. Are there any more bids?" The auctioneer paused. "Done." His chin dipped in a minute nod. "Lot 122-A has been sold to a bidder who has requested that no name be divulged. Thank you very much, ladies and gentlemen. May I now have Lot 123?" An excited buzz filled the room.

Mr. Freshwater leaned over to whisper into Tewksbury's ear, his tone aggrieved, "Can they do that? It sort of takes the fun out of it, doesn't it?"

"It's a fairly common practice, on major items especially. Once a rich man comes to be known as a buyer, he's flooded with sellers day and night. Old J. P. Morgan used to buy through a secret agent who bought through another secret agent—just to avoid that. Our buyer tonight wants to preserve some privacy. I think you'll agree that he's paid for it."

"I guess so. One million, three hundred and seventy thousand dollars for that little desk. And it only had one drawer! Wait till I tell Myra." Freshwater gazed at the professor keenly. "Say, you seem to know quite a lot about all this. There's a little bronze statue coming up soon that I'm supposed to try for. How would you like to bid for me? I mean, would you? Lot 144?"

"I'm afraid not," said Tewksbury. "You see, I've got to get back to Boston, and I've just enough time to get to the airport." The professor smiled. "My family will be expecting me."

"Listen," said Wren, "it was nutty enough when we came down to New York the first time by bus. We only had seventy-one thousand dollars then." She stared out into the night. "It's midnight, for god's sake. Why are you dragging me back to Boston on the midnight bus? We've got one-million-four, nearly, this time. Or hasn't it sunk in yet? I'll buy you a plane, okay? And a matched set of pilots, okay? And where's the professor? Why did he leave so early? Was it because of Swain? What happened to Swain, anyway? And by the way, who bought the goddamn desk? After all this work, I don't even know who—"

Nicholas reached over and placed his hand gently over her mouth. Then he took it away and kissed her softly and sweetly on the lips.

"We have about five or six hours, Redbird, and I want to sit here and tell you why I love you so much. Will you just listen for a while?"

Wren's eyes softened, and she leaned her head on his shoulder.

"Go ahead," she murmured happily. "Tell me."

Twenty-Five

In the pale light of dawn, the misty streets of downtown Boston glistened under the bright lights that lined the way. The bus rolled smoothly into Park Square Station, now almost empty and very quiet.

Their arms around each other's waists, Nicholas and Wren walked slowly through the waiting room toward the line of taxis that stood alongside the curb. One moved to meet them, and they climbed in.

"It's six o'clock in the morning," said Wren. "We danced the whole night through." She sat closer to Nicholas and sighed happily. "Let's buy some stock in Greyhound, Admiral."

"I should have called the professor," said Nicholas.

"You have to stop calling your father 'professor.' It sounds funny."

For a long time they sat silent, listening to the cab's tires hissing along Storrow Drive, toward Cambridge. In the rapidly gathering light of day the Charles River shone like gray steel.

"We'll be there in a few minutes," said Nicholas. "What do we do? Wake him up, or let him sleep?"

"For one million, two hundred and thirty-three thousand bucks—after commission—we let him sleep, pal. For that kind of money, we let *me* sleep too, for a change."

The cab pulled to a gentle stop minutes later, and Nicholas paid the driver. They mounted the front steps together and, quietly as housebreakers, unlocked the front door and eased it slowly open. Down the center hall an oblong of light spilled from an open doorway.

"Nicholas? Wren? Is that you?" called the professor's voice cheerfully. "I'm back here in the kitchen. Coffee's on!"

"It's us," said Nicholas, raising his voice slightly. "Good morning, sir."

"You don't suppose he waited up, do you?" whispered Wren. "What a guy."

They walked into the kitchen. "We came by bus," said Wren, "and it took—" She stopped, her mouth open. "I think I better say what I'm thinking," she said. *"How the fuck did that get here?"*

It was the *bureau du roi*, incongruously placed next to the kitchen sink, its dark golden patina glistening. The letter from Marie Antoinette lay at the exact center, held down by the familiar chamois pouch of jewels.

"I thought you might come by bus," said the old man, "and by George, I was right. As for the desk—it was delivered not an hour ago. One of Mr. Gilliat's vans, you know. Very kind of him, don't you think?"

Nicholas sat down heavily, staring at the professor. He frowned, suddenly remembering. "This estate of yours; the one you said was pretty substantial? *How* substantial, professor? *You* bought the thing, didn't you?" He pulled his hand across his face wearily. "I feel like such a goddamn fool. You must have had a lot of fun watching us make—"

"Turn off the faucet," said Wren briskly. "You just sit there and think for a minute. Don't say something you can't *un*say, right? You can't unring a bell, Nicholas."

His face pale, Nicholas nodded slowly.

"He feels a little upset, professor, Sort of *manipulated,* you might say."

Tewksbury started to respond, but when Wren shook her head vigorously, he subsided obediently.

"Right," said Wren. "I need a cup of coffee. You two masterminds sit there and stare at each other all you want. But I don't want to hear a word out of either of you. Not a word." She bustled to the cupboard and pulled cups and saucers from the shelf, then took spoons from a drawer below and brought them to the table. The clink of plates and cutlery sounded loud in the stillness. Nicholas, sitting across the table from the old man, stared stonily down at his folded hands. The professor's eyes were troubled.

Wren carried the steaming pot from the stove and sat down between them to pour. "Stop staring at your knuckles, Nicholas." She nudged his cup an inch. "Here. Drink it. I want to talk to your father." She lifted her cup and sipped cautiously, then turned to the professor. "He thinks too much, you know. Right now he's got more on his plate than he knows how to say grace over, see? He's dumbfounded. Me, too. We're both dumbfounded. So let me ask you. That desk sold for one million, three-something. It's here, right? So where did you get a million-three? Like Nicholas says, professor, just how big is this estate of yours, anyway? If you don't mind my asking."

Tewksbury shook his head. "The fact is, my dear, that I'm not sure. Mr. Gilpin is working on it."

"Gilpin. Right. So we'll go back and start with *him*. Who is Mr. Gilpin?"

"My lawyer, of course. His firm has handled my affairs for a very long time. I called him up to prepare the papers on this house. You remember, I'm sure. To transfer title to Nicholas and to prepare the adoption papers . . . and . . . and to make some small adjustments in my will. Mr. Gilpin said I would need a statement . . . and that's what he's working on."

"Okay," said Wren. "I follow all that. It has to be a lot of money, though, right? Didn't he say how much? I mean, *roughly?*"

"He did, yes. Perhaps as much as three million dollars, he said. Possibly more." The old man seemed, suddenly, uneasy. "Imagine that," he mumbled.

"I'm trying. Three million dollars. Three *million* dollars. Jee-zuzz. I thought you were a poor young teacher who grew up to be a poor *old* teacher. I mean, would you mind telling us where all that money came from?"

"I *was* a poor young teacher, my dear. Very poor. But I joined the Harvard faculty in 1915. Harvard has always paid its people quite well . . . so that's when I started to invest."

"*Sixty years ago?*"

Tewksbury nodded.

"I don't know much about the stock market, professor. Just bear with me and, like, start at the beginning, okay?"

"There isn't very much to tell, I'm afraid. I was single. My wants have always been very simple, and I had money I could not spend. What to do with it? It seemed to me that our country was strong, and that the thing to do was to invest in companies that were part of that strength."

Wren nodded encouragingly. "That makes sense. What companies?"

"Well, motorcars were beginning to catch on, as I re-

member it. And fuel companies, because motor cars needed fuel. And tires, for the same reason. That sort of thing."

"You mean, like, General Motors and Standard Oil and
Goodyear? Companies like *that*?" There was awe in her
voice.

"Not Goodyear. I liked Mr. Firestone. And then . . .
electricity was also catching on. Steel, too. Very important
to the country, steel was."

"G.E. and U.S. Steel, right? My god."

"Carter Gilpin handled it all; John Gilpin's grandfather.
You have to understand that, my dear. We worked out a
simple plan, actually. Harvard paid me monthly, and I gave
them a standing order to prepare two checks. Half to me, to
live on. Half to Gilpin—to invest. They sent me my check,
they sent him his. When Carter passed on, his son simply
carried on. That was Theodore Gilpin, John's father. It's
John I deal with these days."

"Stocks pay . . . uh . . . dividends, don't they? What
did Carter Gilpin and Theodore Gilpin and John Gilpin do
about *them*?"

"They've always been automatically reinvested."

Wren leaned back in her chair and gave a long, low whistle.

"Telephones?"

The old man nodded.

"Chemicals?"

He nodded again.

"Airplanes?"

"I *think* so. I was a young boy when Wilbur and Orville
Wright made their first flight, you understand. By 1915 air
travel was still a long way off. Years later, I think Theodore
did buy some airline shares. I'm not sure, but I think so."

"Wow. What happened when the stock market crashed?
Didn't it wipe you out?"

Tewksbury smiled for the first time. "Which stock-market crash? We've gone through several, you know. But the country always rights itself. No, we never changed our procedure."

"So you *bought* when the market crashed. Jee-zuzz. Then, everything would go back up again, right?"

"I suppose it did. My arrangement with Gilpin's office was specific, however. I had my work to do, and I didn't want to be distracted with investment questions. Gilpin suggested a fee, and I signed a power of attorney. I suppose it sounds unconventional, foolish perhaps. But they are very upright people, and Carter understood that I cared most about my work. I had my classes and students and research and writing; *they* mattered. I had no wife, no family, and my salary and my pension grew very nicely over the years. The Gilpins have done their part, and I've done mine. That's really all there is to it."

"No statements."

"Never."

Nicholas fiddled with the handle of his cup. "It's really incredible," he murmured. "For instance—you pay income taxes, don't you, sir?" His tone was less strained now, and Wren stifled the impulse to interrupt, quietly crossing her fingers beneath the table.

"Indeed I do pay my income tax, my boy. Mr. Gilpin's office sends me the blank tax forms every year, and I sign them and mail them back. They put in all the numbers. It's much less trouble that way, I've found."

Nicholas rubbed the back of his head.

"I feel a little bit the way I did after Planchet zapped me on the back of the head with that goddamn hammer." A rueful smile worked at his mouth. "You fooled me, professor. You fooled both of us."

The old man leaned forward intently. "Are you sure, my boy? Did I ever say I wanted to make a lot of money? When I joined your gang, what *did* I say I wanted? Adventure,

Nicholas, *adventure!* That was what I needed. I said I was withering away, drying up from boredom. I don't think I fooled you—not in the way I think you mean. What had I to live for, Nicholas? What was left that challenged my vital capacities? When I broke my ankle, you cared. I know you did. But earlier, when I first met you, it was my *spirit* that was almost broken, Nicholas. I told you that. You know I did."

"Well," said Nicholas, "adventures you have had. Not much money to show for it, but lots of adventures."

"To hell with the money," said the old man tartly. "Think about Alexander Peel wrapped in adhesive tape, with Wren's . . . ah . . . intimate wear peeking out of his mouth!"

"Yeah," said Wren, "and Planchet in that grungy priest's gown, blessing the goddamn crowd of reporters in Paris!"

"And trapping Roland Swain with a tape recorder strapped to my leg!" said the professor. He laughed softly.

"Fantastic adventures," murmured Wren. "Really fantastic adventures."

Nicholas pulled at his ear, reflecting.

"Gotcha, Admiral," whispered Wren tenderly. "He's gotcha all the way. Admit it. As long as we live, will we ever forget the picture of poor old Peel with my panties frothing out of his mouth?" She leaned forward and kissed him. "Money or no money, you ran a hell of a gang, Admiral."

"So you had a lot of money and had someone buy the table for you," said Nicholas. "Why? To keep us all out of jail?"

"Certainly not!" said the old man sharply. "Risk is what adventure is all about, isn't it? If your plan hadn't been watertight, we might have drowned at almost any point along the way. We might have been caught. And prosecuted, too. Why, the possibility, the mere possibility, would send those marvelous bubbles of excitement coursing through my blood! No, your plan worked, Nicholas. Take my bidder out of that auction, and *John Kimball* would be looking at that table today!"

"A*ha,*" said Wren. "You wanted to protect Gilliat's then. Was that it?"

"Blether," said Tewksbury. "Harold Gilliat can take care of himself."

"Then . . . why?" said Wren, a touch of confusion in her voice.

The professor stirred his coffee absently. "I'm not sure I can make you understand," he said slowly. "Not because I'm eighty and wise; it isn't that. Perhaps it's the way I've come to look at things—all the beautiful things I've seen and studied and taught. The search for the meaning of beauty has been so much a part of my life. How can I tell you how I feel about the mystery of the creative act that lies hidden in the beautiful things man makes? How can I help you to see it as I have come to see it?"

"Try, sir," said Nicholas softly.

Tewksbury gestured toward the *bureau du roi*. "The world sees it as a *thing,* Nicholas. If it is old and beautiful, it has a price. Often a very high price. But when all is said and done, it remains a thing. But over the years I have come to see beyond the thing, to the human being who created it. A *man* made the original of that desk, Nicholas. An ordinary man, probably. Like you, perhaps. Or me. A man who worked very hard to conceive and design and fashion with his own hands what we see—simply—as an *antique.* But he pursued excellence, I think. And no king could command such a commitment. To tell the world that our clever copy was *his* work was to cheat *him.* No more and no less. And to do it for money seemed to me, at last, brutally unfair."

There was a silence in the kitchen.

"You did it to protect Jean-Henri Riesener," said Nicholas. "I never even *thought* of him."

"Nor did I, at the beginning," said Tewksbury. "Then, as our venture unfolded, a faint sense of discomfort would flow into my mind . . . and I would thrust it away. But back it would come, again and again. Until I understood. I was planning to steal another man's creative commitment . . . and sell it for money. I've told you that money has never been that important to me. I had to buy that table, *because I could not cheat Riesener*. I called my old housekeeper, Bridget Beattie, and briefed her carefully. Then I told Harold Gilliat that Mrs. Beattie would bid for me . . . and the thing was done. I felt a lot better, too, I can tell you."

"*When* did you tell Harold Gilliat?" said Wren suddenly. "I mean, *exactly*."

The professor thought for a moment. "Oh, a minute or two before the Evening Sale commenced. No more."

"Why, that tricky son of a bitch!" said Wren. "He tried to smooch his way to a buy-out! After all our work, *he* was still trying to snatch that table for six hundred lousy thousand dollars! Good night! Who can you trust anymore?"

"Correcto," said Nicholas amiably. "And if Jean-Henri Riesener was sitting in that empty chair, I wonder what he'd be saying? To *us*, I mean? As it is, the professor is out Gilliat's ten-percent commission, and when we get the check, he'll have ninety percent of his money back. Everything considered, it wasn't such a bad deal after all."

"Oh, no," said Wren firmly. "We split three ways. *That's* the deal. I didn't go through all this just to feel a warm glow when I sit by the fire and dream of the good old days when I kicked a guy in the you-know-where. No way. I've had expenses—remember that. I had to throw out those underpants, for one thing. A dead loss. There's about four hundred thousand bucks due me, and I'm taking it. There's another four hundred due you, too, Admiral—and *you're* taking it. The professor here gets his four hundred, so he can give it to Gilpin, who will run it up to three million more for him. And I want my original investment back, too, guys. Let's not get our heads all twisted up, okay?" She frowned at them fiercely. "And one more thing, while I'm at it. I want that genuine fake Caspar Planchet desk brought into the front room. We're going to put a telephone on it and stick a chair in front of it. It's *furniture,* goddamnit."

Tewksbury winked at Nicholas. "She's right, of course."

"I know," said Nicholas.

Epilogue

at Versailles
December 21, 1772

My heart,

It is the time of year for the giving of gifts to those we love, and this little writing table is yours, from me. I write these lines with Venus still moist and my limbs aching sweetly. Last night was magnificent. Before God, I swear that I feel your every inch—and you are every inch my king. I kiss the secret place.

MARIE ANTOINETTE

Riesener, as always, has added our secret drawer.

Nicholas handed the letter to Wren.
"Read it again," he said. "My Turkish pasha just had another idea."